Advance praise for JONATHAN HARPER'S

Daydreamers

"Tenants who destroy your rental apartment, corpses that wash ashore, old men in strip bars, bullies, failed fathers, estranged lovers, and very lost young men negotiating relationships with older ones — welcome to the world of Jonathan Harper's *Daydreamers*, whose assured prose style is turned with deadly accuracy on the crummy, sinister, banality of life in contemporary America. Harper's collection brings to mind a movie of an Anne Tyler novel, if it were directed by David Lynch. There is some original sin at the center of these lost lives. But what is it exactly? Whatever the answer, Harper's stories get better as they accumulate, until they take on the weight of an original artist's vision."

— ANDREW HOLLERAN, author of *Dancer from the Dance*

"A catalog of suburbia's petty desolations and meditations on lost chances; Harper makes for a keen archivist of his characters' flawed, unfinished manifestos."

— GENEVIEVE VALENTINE, author of *The Girls at the Kingfisher Club* and *Mechanique*

"These stories — by turns wry, haunting, and melancholy — examine the ubiquity of loneliness, the painful gaps between yearning and fulfillment, and the myriad difficulties of truly connecting with lovers, family, and friends. Harper's tales have long deserved to be collected under one cover."

— JEFF MANN, author of *Cub* and *Salvation*

"An elegiac, compulsively readable collection of stories about boys, boys, boys — but not the kind you're imagining. Harper writes with simple beauty and heart-breaking depth about young men whose problems and weaknesses lead them to places we, as empathetic readers, can not resist going."

— MATTHEW RETTENMUND, author of *Boy Culture* and *Blind Items*

"Jonathan Harper is a major new talent in fiction — definitely one to watch. His funny, eerie, insightful, wonderfully detailed stories take us home, wherever home may be for us. Harper shows us that we are not alone in our passions, struggles and occasional frustrations, and he does so tenderly, wittily and with great understanding. I am very excited to see what he gives us next!"

— DAVID PRATT, author of *Bob the Book*

"Jonathan Harper's insightful collection is peopled with young, somewhat aimless men struggling to find their place in the world — or doing their best to avoid it. Go-go boys, gamers, or budding artists, they live on the margins, far from the urban sophisticates we're used to seeing in contemporary gay stories. Harper's protagonists wander through bad relationships and bad decisions, gradually piecing themselves together along the way. Their mistakes may be glaring, their stasis occasionally inscrutable, but through complex and empathetic portraits, Harper demonstrates a talent for creating believable characters who linger in the mind long after the page is turned."

— LEWIS DeSIMONE, author of *The Heart's History*

Daydreamers

Jonathan Harper

Daydreamers

Daydreamers

Published in 2015 by Lethe Press, Inc.
118 Heritage Avenue • Maple Shade, NJ 08052-3018 USA
www.lethepressbooks.com • lethepress@aol.com
ISBN: 978-1-59021-296-7 / 1-59021-296-7

"The Bloated Woman" was published in *The Touch of the Sea* (May 2012) and *Best Gay Stories 2013* (June 2013); "The Cake is a Lie" was published in *Chelsea Station* (March 2012); "Costume Dramas" in *Jonathan* under the title "The Rental Unit" (September 2014); "Wallflowers" in *Big Lucks* (January 2015).

These stories are works of fiction. Names, characters, places, and incidents are products of the author's imagination or are used fictitiously.

Set in Agmena and Rechtman.
Interior design: Alex Jeffers.
Interior illustrations: Pierre-Joseph Redouté (1759–1840).
Author photo: Anna Carson DeWitt.
Cover art and design: Nguyễn Thanh Nhàn.

LIBRARY OF CONGRESS CATALOGING-IN-PUBLICATION DATA
Harper, Jonathan (Storyteller)
[Short stories. Selections]
Daydreamers / Jonathan Harper.
   pages cm
ISBN 978-1-59021-296-7 (pbk. : alk. paper)
1. Short stories, American. I. Title.
PS3608.A7735D37 2015
813'.6--dc23
               2014046726

Dedicated to Michelle Weiss Hilburn,
with much love and admiration.

Acknowledgments

$\mathcal{F}$irst, thank you so much to Steve Berman and Lethe Press for taking a chance on me. This wouldn't have happened without you. Also, thank you to the amazing editors, Alex Jeffers and Adam Robinson, who both helped me get my shit together.

Much appreciation to the MFA Program at American University, the Writer's Colony at Dairy Hollow and the Virginia Center for the Creative Arts. Also to the fine publications *Big Lucks*, *Chelsea Station*, *Jonathan* and the *Best Gay Stories* series, in which some of these stories appeared.

There are too many people I want to recognize here for their encouragement, support and kindness. This is just a start:

Nicholas Benton, Nicholas Boggs, Linda Caldwell, Philip Clark, Halley Cohen, Mark Cugini, Jameson Currier, Crescent Dragonwagon, Danielle Evans, Daphne Gottlieb, Stephanie Grant, Andrew Holleran, David Keplinger, Anne Lacy, Eileen Lavelle, EJ Levy, Jeff Mann, Jim Marks, Richard McCann, Heather McDonald, Jeff Middents, Denise Orenstein, Greta Schuler, Mary Switalski, Ginger Walker and Melissa Wyse.

To Don Rhodes and Matt Hilburn. You guys left the party way before your time and I wish you were still here because I have something neat to show you. I miss you both.

Thank you to my wonderful family for putting up with me.

And most of all, thank you to my wonderful husband, Gordon Phelps. You continue to inspire me every day.

Contents

Repossession

No one knew exactly what Amber was doing in Fayetteville or where she'd come from. According to the rumors, the kind she'd likely started herself, she had been a successful engineer up until her accident. Now, she received checks from her disability pension and supposedly earned commissions from consulting jobs. There was a lot of speculation over the details of her accident. She wore an eyepatch over the right side of her face but refused to acknowledge it. Whenever someone asked, she changed the subject into some vivid story about her old burlesque troupe or the time Gore Vidal himself had complimented her at a dinner party. Women found her irreverent, men desired her and every bartender in Cumberland County seemed to owe her a favor.

So when Randal moved back into his brother's house for the fourth time, it amused him that Tom, prudish boring Tom, was bunking up with such an exotic lady companion. On one hand, Randal felt a sort of camaraderie with her. They were both heavy drinkers, vulgar storytellers and he assumed she was the type of woman who would unite with him against Tom and together they could pull out whatever was plugged up his tightly wound ass. On the other hand, Randal didn't trust her. It wasn't her tall tales or her mysterious finances. There was something territorial, almost predatory, about her and the way her lone eye examined you as if scanning for a weakness.

The day Randal had shown up on his brother's doorstep, carrying two overstuffed suitcases, he had prepared himself for one of Tom's lectures about responsible living. Instead, he was introduced to Amber. She gave a bemused smile while her evil eye assessed him. He knew he looked ridiculous to her: seersucker shorts with a dirty blazer over his tank top. His hair was a spiky mess from the long train ride down. After a prolonged silence, she poured each of them a drink and said, "Welcome to our home," pronouncing the operative word, "our," as if she was prepared to defend it. Apparently she knew all about Randal's habit of rushing off to New York. How he'd crash and burn until his savings ran out before sauntering home to Tom until he was ready to try again.

It was a cycle she seemed determined to break.

So it did not surprise him when after three months, a mere visit in Randal-time, Tom entered the guestroom and asked him to move out. "It's time to stop dicking around," Tom said, scratching his arm nervously. "You're getting too old to rely on me to take care of you. You need to grow where you're planted. That means being independent and living within your means."

Randal kept his mouth shut, refused to give anyone the satisfaction of an argument. Amber was obviously behind this decision. He'd been expecting it. Back in New York, a psychic had warned him that his brother was susceptible to negative influences, that a she-devil was in his future and her game was sabotage.

The next morning, he found Amber waiting in the kitchen. She narrowed her eye at him as she greased up a frying pan. He was a little hung over and aching and even worse, he'd awoken to a sticky dampness in his underpants. At twenty-eight, Randal Moyer had a wet dream and there was his brother's girlfriend glaring at him as if she had firsthand knowledge of it.

"Your alarm was going off for an hour," she said flatly. "What the hell?"

"Why didn't you wake me?" he asked. Then he averted his eyes. The deep *V* of Amber's shirt had dipped dangerously low over her chest, causing the pink mound of her nipple to poke out.

"Your door was locked. I was ready to take it off the hinges." Amber was blunt like that. And unforgiving. She dropped a few strips of bacon in the skillet, too tough to care that her nipple practically dangled over the hot oil. Randal imagined her eyepatch gently gliding down to cover it. "Are you going to need help finding an apartment?" she asked.

"I'll be fine," he said.

"Well, good. You always seemed resourceful enough." She cracked two eggs into the pan. "I have to admit, we feel a little guilty about putting you on the spot like this. But trust me when I say this isn't about you. We need our space."

Randal shrugged. He felt nauseated from the previous night's anger drinking. The smell of frying meat didn't help either. He sucked in a breath to subdue it, but Amber must have misinterpreted his hesitation because she tensed up fiercely, free hand hoisted to her hip, eye focused and, finally, her boob jiggled completely out of her shirt.

"I'm having a baby. Tom doesn't want anyone to know till after the first trimester. But I figured you deserved an explanation." The eggs and bacon sizzled. "You bounce around too much and that gets tiring for everybody. You need to get settled into something permanent. That way, we can all move on with our lives."

His head filled with a sleepy type of hurt. It all didn't make sense. So Amber was pregnant and that meant *he* was the one who had to settle down? Get settled and end up like his brother? The very idea of it was degrading. Growing up, Tom had been a science genius, talked incessantly about space travel and working for NASA. Now, he was a high school chemistry teacher and propped himself up on a martyr's pedestal over it. But as Randal saw it Tom hadn't just settled — he'd given up. What did chemistry have to do with spaceships anyway?

"I was planning on moving back to New York," he said.

Amber didn't lose her pose. She knew her boob was still hanging out and winced as a speck of oil hit it. She didn't care. "If you can make it work, then you have my blessings. But try convincing Tom you won't show up on our doorstep in another few months. There isn't enough room here for four." She scooped out one of the eggs, now burnt, and slid it onto a small dish. She grimaced as she poked the remaining contents of the skillet. "Since you're here, you want some breakfast?"

"Can't. I'm late for work," he said, ignoring the charred egg. But before he left, he yelled out, "Oh Amber, put your tit away before you burn it off!" The front door closed in time enough to deflect the spatula she threw at him.

*A*n hour later, he sat shotgun in Winston's tow truck watching the bland ugliness of Fayetteville zip by in a long iridescent blur. They passed graffiti-covered buildings, the military base and the neon sign of the Lucky Mao's Chinese Restaurant Emporium. Winston himself was even drifting off in some farscaped daydream. The heat and humidity was enough to make them almost forget. Forget about work protocols and the two-week long search for the infamous Mercedes that evaded them on every drive.

Randal had worked for the towing company on and off for years. It was a humbling experience to return. His co-workers were tough-skinned men who over time had developed a soft spot for the little oddity amongst them. Randal was always paired up with old Winston, who was the least judgmental, and sent back out onto the monotonous routes of apartment complexes and office parks, scouting for cars without decals to tow back to the automobile graveyard. The real money, however, came from the repo orders. For those poor souls who defaulted on their loans, Winston and Randal would pay a visit, slap some paperwork in their hands and confiscate the vehicle. The banks took care of the rest and paid a hefty finder's fee to the lucky towers who got their hands on the merchandise. You always worked in pairs in this business, one to drive the tow, the other to drive the repossessed car. It was depressing work, a low building fever of guilt mixed with a few drops of competition that all the collectors suffered. But then, Fayetteville was a depressing town burdened with sluggish heat and a bunch of lifers who talked about nothing but getting out.

They approached an oblong glass building that housed a real estate agency. The Mercedes belonged to a Realtor, one of those fast-talking hustlers who spiked up the market by convincing people their houses were worth more than what was reasonable. His waxy face appeared on billboards and newspaper ads everywhere, always smiling with the confidence of a man who wasn't six months behind on car payments. But despite his public persona, he was invisible; he'd successfully dodged every tow truck for weeks.

After a few laps around the lot, Randal said, "Pull up front and I'll go inside." His clipboard was out and ready for action, but the tow didn't stop.

"No, sir. Either he's out or else he knows better than to bring it here," Winston replied. He brushed a few rogue hairs from his eyes.

"Pull over. I'm going right up to his desk and let him know we mean business."

But the tow truck grumbled back onto the main road as Winston shook his head. "Try not to take too much pride in your work," he said. At heart Winston considered himself a man of old hippie principles. He needed this job but still took every opportunity to rebuke it. "There ain't nothing charitable about what we do for a living," he often said. "That's not something to be proud of."

*D*uring these drives, Randal would fantasize about New York where being young and poor was practically a virtue. As long as you looked young enough and not too hardened from the experience, it was easy to find some older gentleman to pay for dinner. Most recently, he had interned for a fledgling literary press situated in a dirty office above a convenience store. His desk was surrounded by uncorked wine bottles, ashtrays and lofty piles

Jonathan Harper

of paper. No one ever seemed to work, yet every few weeks he held the latest copy of a glossy poetry book they had managed to scrape together. Even his housing situation was on the pleasant side of poverty: a one-bedroom apartment he shared with two girls, a blonde club promoter and a Korean fashion design student. Together, they had stayed up until sunrise eating bowls of kimchi, snorting lines of coke and discussing their various affairs. Some nights they dared long-winded conversations about their budding careers. The blonde girl would chug her tea, eyes bloodshot, and say, "One day you'll be publishing your own magazine and writing features for *The Village Voice*. And you'll be showcasing kimonos at Fashion Week." Then she'd squeal, "Now tell me about my career!"

Yet a career always eluded him. Money disappears quickly when you aren't making any.

They chalked a few tires in an apartment complex before pulling in to the Lighthouse Diner. It was a long chrome structure that looked like a giant silver turd left out to sizzle. But the portions were generous and the waitresses didn't care how much coffee you drank as long as you'd let them sneak out back for a smoke once in a while. Winston ordered his usual plate of steak and eggs, cheese grits and buttered toast.

"I'll bring the rest out when you're done, you glutton," the waitress said.

"Stay close." Winston gave her a wink. For a while, he'd had his eye on that Spanish beauty, Carmen, who worked the register. But if any one of the ladies suggested grabbing a beer after shift he'd happily oblige them. Across the booth, Randal brooded over the local newspaper spread out on the Formica. His eyes went back and forth. The pages first, then out the diner window at passing traffic. "You're a million miles away," Winston said, braced for whatever emotional discharge was coming.

"I'm getting evicted." Randal gave an angry rendition of the previous night, ending with Amber's confession that morning. "She's like a succubus. She's got her claws into my brother and wants me out of the picture. And for what?"

Winston crossed his arms like a genie. He knew his comrade was hung over and prone to exaggeration. He also knew that Little Randy Moyer was a well-bred pain in the ass with high goals but without the logical mind to reach them. If some people were meant to do and act, then people like Randy were

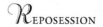

meant to feel and think and experience. Unfortunately, those types rarely got what they wanted.

"I don't think I know what a succubus is, but I'm not quite sure it's accurate."

"I was saving up my money to get out of here. They both knew that," Randal said.

"Yup. It's a bloody shame," Winston said. "But were you paying them rent?"

"I helped out."

"Were you on a lease?"

"No."

"Then technically speaking you weren't evicted."

Randal went silent, bit off a chunk of bagel and chewed it slowly. They were quiet for several minutes, breathing in the fumes of the deep fryer while Tammy Wynette sang on the jukebox. When he felt they'd loitered enough, Winston paid their check. Then he turned to find his partner hoisting up a page from the newspaper. Randal's mood had visibly improved in a matter of seconds.

"We're in luck," he said. "There's an open house down the road from here." His finger pointed to a square advertisement of a beautiful brick cottage, price reduced. The Realtor's face sat smugly in the bottom corner with a smile that hinted he could sell off your own children for the right price.

There was heavy traffic at the open house and again Winston insisted they not cause an unnecessary disturbance. He pulled the tow truck onto an adjacent street and shook his head pitifully as Randal pulled out a pair of heavy binoculars from his backpack.

"What are you doing with those? Bird watching?"

"If we're going into stealth-mode, then we must be prepared."

Winston sighed. At least Randal was returning to his usual mischievous self. "Those aren't subtle." And then, even though he already knew the answer, Winston asked, "Where the hell did you get those things?"

"Borrowed them from Tom."

They walked briskly around the neighborhood checking for the Mercedes before taking a vantage point on the edge of a playground. They were uphill with a clear view of the entire street. Below them, the open house looked more like a garden party; the Realtor had tied balloons to the welcome sign as potential buyers stood in small clusters, sipping from paper cups and read-

ing fliers. Winston lit a cigarette and watched his partner squat low to the ground, half concealed by the bushes, binoculars staring ahead.

"You are not subtle," Winston reminded him.

"Get down! I see him. He's right there on the front porch."

Winston took a long drag and locked eyes with a passing elderly couple. They were walking along the edge of the playground, tilting their heads in a confused manner. Winston waved and they returned the favor as they continued their march further up the hill.

As he crouched, Winston felt a vein twitch along his temple. "Do you see the Mercedes or not?"

"Hard to tell from this angle." Randal continued his surveillance with vigor. The luxury cars blended together in the brutal sunlight; it felt impossible to distinguish any of them. His eyes settled on a young couple, the wife very pregnant. She rubbed her swollen belly as her husband fanned her. They were sharing a moment, her mouth pursing into a coy smile while her husband examined the listing. Though he could not tell why, Randal felt utter contempt for this happy, boring couple. He stood up through a head rush, brushed off the yellow blades of grass. "What would you say if I asked to crash with you for a while?"

Winston gave a solemn nod, as if he'd previsioned this. "I'd say something like, there would have to be a lease involved." Then, he pointed down towards the open house. The Realtor, having hooked his tendrils into the pregnant couple, led them to a black Volkswagen on the corner and pulled out a briefcase from the backseat. Winston let out a grunt. "It ain't here. Time to move on."

*F*urther down the boulevard, they entered a townhouse development. The Realtor lived in the center and, as expected, the Mercedes was nowhere in sight.

"Not sure why we bother," Winston said. "No use searching for something that don't want to be found."

He had barely tapped the accelerator when suddenly Randal clutched his arm and yelled out, "Stop the truck!" It gave Winston an awful fright. The tow came to an abrupt halt while the poor man clutched his chest. In any other case, he would have grabbed Randal by the neck, squeezed, shook and repeated. But there it was, the Mercedes, discreetly camouflaged on a side street between two pickup trucks. It had been painted a glossy champagne color, which accentuated two triangular dents along the driver's side, looking like mechanical bite marks. The side-view mirror had been knocked clean off at the hilt.

Winston just shook his head. "Such a shame to treat a lady this way. She deserved better." As they rolled up, Randal matched the license plate against the repo order. It was their Mercedes. The long search was over.

"Let's hook her up and get out of here," Randal said.

Winston scratched through his whiskers. "Slow down there, buddy. She's sandwiched in good. No way we're towing her without scraping things up further." He threw the stick in reverse and rolled back up to the townhomes. "Let's do this right. Follow procedure."

If a door is an indication of the inhabitants inside, then this door was misleading. It was painted glossy red with a brass pineapple-shaped knocker. It was the kind of impression Realtors relied on: two universal signs of welcoming. After a doorbell ring and a knock, it opened to an attractive middle-aged woman, the Realtor's wife. Her top lip was brutally thick, her face almost too narrow for it. Both ends of her mouth slurred downward as Randal handed her the paperwork.

"What happens now?" Her entire presence was defined by that mouth: a pair of floating red lips atop a lady's body.

Randal maintained a stoic composure, the kind he'd seen Winston use a dozen times before. "It's best if you sign the order. We'll let you collect your personal belongings and then we'll drive it to the lot."

"And if I don't sign?"

"Your other option is to call your bank and see if they'll accept immediate payment. Otherwise, we'll tow your car."

The Lip Lady grimaced but remained composed. "I need to call my husband," she said.

"That's fine, but we are ordered to take the car. If you give me your keys now, we'll wait until you've spoken with him." She nodded and closed the door in his face, the brass pineapple glimmering in the sunlight.

$\mathcal{B}$ack at the truck, it was hot enough to scorch the taste buds off your tongue. Randal swigged from his water bottle and swished the lukewarm metallic flavor around his mouth before spitting it out. He calculated his next few paychecks and added it to the meager sum in his bank account.

Jonathan Harper

It was enough to hide away for a week somewhere up north, but not good for much else.

"Been ten minutes," Winston said. "Don't take that long to get keys."

The front curtains of the townhome rustled as the Lip Lady peered out at them.

"That's it. Let's hook her up and get out of here," Randal said.

Winston didn't respond. He was staring at another tow truck rumbling down the street. "Here comes trouble," he said and reversed out to block the other guy from moving forward. The wreckers made a *T* in the middle of the road. "You go up there and you get those keys before these knuckleheads try to stake a claim," Winston ordered and Randal hopped out.

Even though Fayetteville was a sprawling town, there were never enough bounties to go around evenly. All the repo men knew each other and carved out loosely defined territories. They might drink together and watch each other's backs, but when it came to a collection all pleasantries quickly dissipated. Out of the other truck came Alvarez, a walking cartoon depiction of some circus strongman: bronze skin, bald head, mustache and two ballooning arms that looked ready to snap a metal pole in half. It was well speculated that Alvarez was looking to change up towing partners and had a special gleam in his eye for little Randy. Their coworkers compared it to a grown man trying to cuddle a puppy. Even the most pungent-spirited men seemed to approve of the pairing.

As Randal knocked again on the Lip Lady's door, he kept an eye on the commotion down by the trucks.

"We were here first," he heard Winston saying.

"Be reasonable." Alvarez spat out a loogie. "This neighborhood's been on our route for months."

"His office is in our jurisdiction, so we got just as much claim as you."

Both men knew that in the time it would take Winston to maneuver his truck around, Alvarez's partner could whip theirs around the block and they'd be at a similar standoff. The only hope was Randal, still knocking at the door. If he could get the repo order signed, the stalemate would be over.

Of course, it is a much advertised feature of townhomes that they come with a standard back entrance, usually a sliding glass door off the kitchen or in the basement. These doors are quiet and discreet, especially when you have a nuisance waiting out front. But these are the commonplace things one forgets when the mind melts from heatstroke.

REPOSESSION

As Randal kept knocking and glancing back, it was the logical progression of things that the Lip Lady put on her sneakers, grabbed her purse and quietly walked out through this back entrance. The way they remembered it, especially Randal, was that it happened in the same blurry motion of a desert mirage. The Mercedes suddenly pulled out of its hiding place and glided forward. All the repo men found themselves dumbly staring forward as it sped off while its fat-lipped driver yelled out, "So long, suckers!"

They repossessed another car that afternoon: a fancy little Miata from a college-aged boy. It was a sad affair made worse by the parents observing from the sidelines. At least the boy had dignity. He signed the order and surrendered his keys without a hint of protest. Even as he emptied his trunk, he kept apologizing to no one in particular.

Afterwards, Randal drove the Miata back through town. It was nice to feel alone, even if it was in someone else's car. The college student had looked on the verge of tears by the time they left. He had looked at his father with the sad acknowledgement that he had failed at something. Randal almost felt pity for the boy, but this was the nature of the business and people were cheated out of what life owed them all the time. And yet, he thought, wouldn't it be nice to see that very look on Amber's face? What if she were behind on a few of her payments?

Winston was waiting for him at the auto graveyard. "Took the long way back, huh?"

"I needed time to think."

Winston nodded. "I believe it." And with his usual empathy for the unfortunate, he declared they both needed a break and would take a few days off to recover.

It was customary after a hard day's work for repo men to convene on Winston's back patio and get drunk. If the front porch light was on, it meant the grill was lit and visitors were welcome. People would show up out back, drink by the fire pit and take turns pissing in the cluster of chalk maples that stood just beyond the patio. By morning they typically discovered some poor fool who had passed out in the bushes, pants still unzipped and snoring.

But before any of that could get started, Winston showed Randal his spare room. It was narrow with dingy carpet and a twin bed. "It isn't much, but the

Jonathan Harper

fan works and the closet's decent. Plus you're close to the kitchen," he said. He typed up a makeshift lease on his computer: two hundred a month, half utilities and the right to terminate with a full month's notice. "I'll give you some time to muse it over," and then he flipped on the porch light and went out back.

Alone, Randal felt a sickly indignation about living here. The house had originally been owned by Winston's dead sister and little had been changed since her passing. It was a descent into a frilly pink hell with floral wallpaper and Precious Moments figurines. Edna had a mythic reputation as a foul-mouthed harpy for the forces of good who spent her final days double-fisting her oxygen tank and menthol cigarettes. Winston had moved down from Vermont to take care of her and now that she was gone he had been trying to close down her estate for years, still paying the mortgage and making no progress towards selling. To Randal it was a shame to waste his New York money on rent in this place, but it seemed too good a deal to pass up.

Not knowing what to do, Randal called his brother's phone. And when Tom didn't answer, he called again. This time, Amber picked up.

"What is it?" She made labored breaths as if she was running a marathon.

"Hand it over to Tom, please," Randal said.

"Well, he's a little indisposed at the moment," and then she started to giggle. That's when Randal became well aware of the expended energy taking place on the other side of the phone. It was a horrible noise, like someone trying to squeeze into pants that no longer fit.

"Just tell him I have news…"

There was a small commotion and Amber said something away from the receiver, "Wait a sec. Stop." Then her voice was clear. "Is this the type of news I would approve of?"

"I won't be home for dinner." He hung up before she could reply. Just the sound of Amber's voice was enough to make his blood boil, but to have her interrogate him while mid-coitus? That was disgusting. He suddenly wanted to punch something. Instead he grabbed the lease, signed it and threw the pen across the room. He'd rather sleep on the streets than share the same roof with her. And if he regretted this hasty decision later, then it would obviously be her fault.

By the time Randal made it to the patio the hazy light of evening was overhead. Men from the towing company were settled into their first round of beers as Winston poured charcoal into his rusted grill. Already, they were grumbling over the day's work. Someone belched to a small applause. Two sturdy women stood on the side, one holding a tub of potato salad and the other cradling a plastic bottle of cheap bourbon. And then, there was Alvarez sitting quietly in the back. He glanced up at Randal and gave a quick nod to the empty chair beside him.

"My brother kicked me out." Randal said this with the annoyed inflection of someone who had already been asked about it one too many times. "But I'm sure it was Amber's doing. She's had it out for me since day one."

Alvarez downed his beer, crunched the can with barely a gesture, and then reached for another. "Do you got someplace to go?"

"Marcy, check this shit out," said the lady with the potato salad. "I swear, you put two of those types in one place and they're bound to end up together. Just you watch." Several of the guys nervously chuckled their agreement and the other woman, Marcy, called it "sweet". Then the subject was dropped as quickly as it had come up. Randal already sensing Alvarez retract inside himself a little further; he'd stay quiet all night if they let him.

"If you're going to stay here, you'll need to learn how to work the grill," Winston called out and Randal sighed. The bourbon was making its way around and Alvarez was still giving him an eyeful, but instead he moved into the heat of the grill and took command of the tongs. "Don't you worry," Winston said with a wink. "He's not going anywhere."

Within minutes they smelled of charcoal and charred beef while the banter and the drinking escalated. As Randal attempted his first flip, the hamburger meat broke apart.

"That'll never do," Winston said. "You really are a city boy."

One of the lookers tossed her hair before lighting a Parliament. "Don't mind us, we're only starving over here." This inspired a series of heckles, and Randal cursed loudly as a second piece of undercooked meat broke off and fell into the smoking embers.

"Goddamn everything!" he snapped with a foot stomp.

Winston just laughed and resumed governorship of the grill. "Sorry your life's a wreck. But then, we're in the business of wrecking lives."

"You should feel sorry you don't have any steak sauce. How am I supposed to eat this shit?"

With the burgers served, the conversation dimmed down. Winston pulled out his ukulele and plucked a few chords. Most of them had bridged into the

mellow side of intoxication where they were comfortable, but not much else. Only the women were talking and laughing, mostly in deprecating humor regarding their company. Ladies didn't stick around long on the back patio, as Winston's cookouts had a habit of attracting the over-worked and broken-hearted. Two of the men were reminiscing over a sweet little honey they had both pursued for a good year before she took off with a captain at Fort Bragg. Now, an army wife, she sent them German postcards signed with *x*'s and *o*'s, neither man quite sure how they'd allowed this to happen.

"Serves you right," Marcy said. "That girl was half your age. You guys always chase after what you can't have."

"Come on, keep it friendly," Alvarez muttered.

"I'm serious," she said. "There's a pair of real women here and nobody's thought to ask either of us what we're doing later tonight." The ladies let out a phlegm-filled laugh while the men shrugged in agreement.

But Randal didn't know what was so funny. He had forsaken his dinner in favor of the unguarded bourbon, drinking in steady gulps to the point where he'd gag. His thoughts were drunk-driving through an array of disappointments, like the elusive Mercedes and the rented room off Winston's kitchen. That stupid lease felt signed in his own blood. What lay ahead were endless nights on the patio, surrounded by unhappy workers and lion-hearted women, all drinking away their frustrations. Even now that Winston was trying to woo Marcy with a few plucked chords aimed at her heart, she played coy, letting out an exasperated sigh. Even Alvarez seemed too ambivalent, one moment coiled up in his own introversion, the next adjusting himself to be more visible. If Randal said, "Get me out of here," he knew Alvarez would take him anyplace he wanted to go, but afterwards, what would be left to fantasize about?

He wanted to drink like he didn't know any better. That was one of his habits that Tom criticized. "You don't need a drink," Tom often said. That was the constant debate: to need or to want. As Randal sat there, nearing the end of his bottle, it became clear to him that he needed to go speak with his brother. He began mentally rehearsing a long-winded explanation of his own shortcomings and his vow to work harder towards something more permanent. And then Amber came into his mind, her eye narrowed into a conduit of evil. He wanted to warn his brother that the world was an unfair, merciless place, that there were no true opportunities left and, worst of all,

the person who lies and tells you there are is sometimes the same person sitting there in your house claiming she has your baby in her belly.

He rose and staggered into the house, retrieved the keys to Winston's truck from the ceramic ashtray on the counter. Their shiny metal teeth gleamed in his hand like vengeance; he felt them bite the soft part of his palm as he walked through the front door. Outside, it was dark. Fireflies danced over the front lawn while the yellow light from the street lamps made the whole neighborhood appear as false as a film set. That morning he had not known he was going to tow Amber's crusty old Buick, but the moment the thought came to mind it was as if it had always been there, a mean little spirit that sat waiting for the right moment to strike. This opportunity wouldn't present itself again, so he dashed out across the lawn and cursed when he fumbled the keys just before the truck door.

"What the hell are you doing?" Winston bellowed.

Too much drinking had created a sort of tunnel vision. Randal was so focused on the task at hand that he almost misunderstood the question. He was about to yell back, "I'm going to teach her a lesson," when he realized that Winston was sprinting towards him and Alvarez was cautiously peering out the door. Randal hadn't even unlocked the truck when Winston cuffed his arm. The grip was tight, authoritative, and Randal found the touch so offensive it almost burned and he shoved the old man back with an unintended force that sent poor Winston stumbling over the curb. They exchanged a brief look, Winston's mouth agape. Out of instinct, Randal pulled open the driver side door, not quite sure of what had just happened, but knowing he had to get away. As he crawled inside, Alvarez wrapped both arms around his waist, pulled him away from the truck while Randal kicked out at the air. Across the street some woman stood out on the porch, peering through the twilight to get a better look.

"Ease down," Alvarez said.

Winston rose slowly, face as hot as light bulbs. "You're too drunk to be driving anywhere. What the fuck do you think you're doing?" he said before turning away to regain his composure. The rest of the drinkers came sulking around the corner, their curiosity and contempt radiating off of them. Randal felt it building up. First a single frustrated tear, then the open sobs as Alvarez tightened his grip — it was an odd mixture of subjugation and comfort. It felt like the embrace was squeezing the anger out from within him. But then, even if someone had bothered to ask, he wouldn't have known

Jonathan Harper

what exactly he was crying over. It had something to do with New York and Amber, his horrible job, the next week and all the weeks to come after.

Winston shooed the onlookers back to the patio, then flipped off the nosy neighbor. He stood still, stoic even, waiting patiently for his new tenant to settle down. "And where were you planning on going?" he asked.

"To see my brother," Randal's face buckled as Alvarez let go.

"What were you planning to do when you got there?"

"I wanted to talk to him." Randal looked further down the street where it faded into darkness, a long road to nowhere speckled with lamplights and fireflies. He felt depleted. "I was going to tow Amber's car. She deserves it."

Alvarez moved aside, lit a smoke and when Winston gave him a nod he turned and followed the others.

"Please don't go," Randal thought, but his voice was lost. He waited for some force of punishment, perhaps a punch in the gut or at least a good reprimand, but nothing happened. When he finally looked up, he felt caught in Winston's eyes — gray as ash, puffy with long crow's-feet. They looked so old and vulnerable, yet full of the wisdom that came from years of experience. In that moment Winston appeared almost sage-like.

"You really are a stupid boy, aren't you?" he said.

Randal nodded. He was in complete agreement.

Nature

The suspensions took place in a small warehouse in the back end of a derelict strip mall. Developers had once scavenged the area, all of Sterling for that matter. They bought out half the businesses before abandoning their great renovation plans altogether, and left behind a wasteland. Most of the storefronts sat like vacant black holes of disrepair. The only signs of life came from the Sunoco, the Lebanese deli and the tattoo parlor on the corner — the sole business left with access to the warehouse.

August had never witnessed the suspensions. Until recently he had no way of knowing such things actually happened. He was a lithe twenty-three year old, self-conscious about his effeminate mannerisms and in love with the most distant intangible things. He regarded the suspensions with the same fascination he had for the constellations. They were in a different plane of existence to him.

His cousin, Libby, was a co-owner of the Paradise Ink tattoo parlor, a bento box of small curtained alcoves and corridors. The foyer was a mixture of white and chrome with loud glossy tiles reminiscent of a hospital waiting room. Laminated prints of ink designs covered the walls; the glass case of the register counter displayed water pipes beneath a handwritten sign, *For Tobacco Use Only*. Because of the neighborhood demolition, business had slowed down to a trickle and the few regulars left mostly came to socialize or buy drugs from the staff. August came at least three evenings a week, taking the bus down after his classes at the tech school let out. These regular visits had made him into a permanent fixture. And if the staff did not like it, they at least accepted it with the tenderness of taking in a stray kitten.

Libby came in each night after her day job to do the bookkeeping, inventory or some other desperately important project the staff neglected. She would scamper doe-like between the register and the back office, arms full of small binders, her linen skirts swishing against her calves. August would sit and stare at his cousin with juvenile fascination. Then his mind would unravel into a hazy fantasy of a large sky full of puffy clouds, Libby's body dangling underneath them like a marionette, her hair veiling her face, her mouth quivering. When Libby caught his gaze, the image would disappear. She would smile coyly at him, as if she guarded a wonderful secret.

They had grown up together in Massachusetts. When he thought of home, it was a flood of loathsome memories: ugly duplex houses and Catholic churches, the endless family obligations that governed his life. The Aunts, of that old Irish stock, all lived within a few blocks of each other and kept their families close; Wilford was like a cocoon. Only Libby had made it bearable. She had been a reckless young heathen who toted him around like a favorite rag doll. He was seven when she first started taking him on night drives into Boston. He was twelve on the night of her engagement party, both of them drinking from a champagne bottle long after everyone else had gone to bed. When Libby married and departed for law school, he spent years clinging to a dim hope that her absence was all a ruse and that she was somewhere in hiding, plotting his rescue as well.

He had followed her down to Virginia because his life in Wilford had broken down in a terrible way. A year ago he was a college drop-out who kept boomeranging back to his parents' house, stuck on antidepressants, the Aunts constantly monitoring him. While it was difficult to think of a specific example, he felt subjected to an endless string of indignities. The last was being fired from his job at a hole-in-the-wall restaurant. The chef's wife had been running her mouth all over town that August was having an affair with her husband.

So it did not surprise him to come home one evening and find all five of the Aunts holding court. These types of meetings were not uncommon — there was always family business to discuss. They perched around the living room, cradling their tea cups with furrowed concentration as his mother tried to lead him upstairs.

"He can't stay here," one of them said and another one added, "Of course not. Who will hire him now?"

He felt baited by this preposterous idea that you could be banished from a place you despised. The Aunts had that kind of authority, whether they had earned it or not, and continued on as if they hadn't seen him. It was Aunt Paula, the diplomatic one, who calmly reminded the tribunal that they had once held similar conversations over Libby. Yet somehow she had managed to prosper. He could go live with her, go back to school. She would be a good influence, they all agreed.

Jonathan Harper

$\mathcal{L}$ibby was starting over as well. Her marriage had been a short-lived catastrophe that led to her present state as a divorced, childless woman in her thirties. She had not only welcomed this change but felt rejuvenated by it. She was a tall, almost spidery woman who wore horn-rimmed glasses and was prone to loud bursts of energy and ideas. "I am finally coming into my power," she had said, even if she didn't know what to do with it.

When she bought into the tattoo parlor, Libby had intended to be a silent partner. But without her bookkeeping skills Trevor would have run it into the ground long ago. Sometimes she regretted going into business with him, but then Trevor was ingrained so heavily into her life that it seemed impossible not to. He was a longtime friend, now housemate, congenial and low maintenance. While he had little brains for business, he made up for it with enthusiasm. It didn't hurt that he was also ruggedly handsome and genuinely enjoyed having August around. This gave extra incentive to keep Paradise Ink afloat.

The three would often sit in the break room for hours past closing, drinking whiskey from Styrofoam cups, and jokingly complain about the business. Libby often ranted about the developers driving away clientele, how Sterling was a dying town and could not be revived. Trevor, on the other hand, was always scheming about the back warehouse. So far he'd rented it out for a private party, an art gallery and for the suspensions. This usually escalated into a brief fight, Libby arguing such events cost more money than they brought in while Trevor refused to take her seriously. Then they would take their argument to the office, only to return a short time later, silent and disheveled. August would observe this routine with a pang of affection. He had caught Trevor at home as well, one morning, sneaking out of the master bedroom, naked and sweaty, penis dangling like a pendulum. An unspoken camaraderie had grown between them, partly because of August's timid nature and Trevor's need to scandalize him. Trevor would often strut by, proudly flash his genitals as August pretended not to look. And then came the invitations to join in whatever took place in the back warehouse, though they were never followed through on because Libby declared it off limits.

$\mathcal{T}$he day it finally happened was a Sunday, the Lord's day, and it came with little warning. At first August was in a state of ghastly anxiety. He had not slept the night before, still felt sluggish and unprepared when he finally left the house. A late cold front had left ice on the sidewalks. He nearly fell twice walking to the bus stop. He took the bus down, bundled in his coat, eating hash brown nuggets from a greasy fast-food bag. Before he reached Paradise Ink, he passed a handful of day workers huddled at the edge of a U-haul store and a homeless man who presented a shaky open palm. "I got nothing," August told him and then, feeling guilty, he added, "I'm a paycheck away from being in your spot."

"Jesus loves you," the man said, wavering, as the day workers kept their distance.

When he entered Paradise Ink, he could hear the humming of a tattoo gun from behind one of the curtained alcoves — at least they had a customer. Libby was in her usual manic jog between the cash register and the office. She looked perturbed, eyes dilated to the semblance of some exasperated Anime character. "What are you doing here?" she asked without speaking and just as August's smile faded she spun back towards the office.

$\mathcal{N}$ick was the only other full-time employee at Paradise Ink, a mediocre tattoo artist with poor work ethic who had been lurking in Trevor's shadow for years. He was an ogre of a man, well over six feet tall, with a large balding skull and red muttonchops that distracted from his sagging neck. Back in the city, he had enjoyed the notoriety of being an old guard of the scene, a regular presence in the alternative nightclubs that kept shutting down. When he spoke of them it was with disgruntled nostalgia for the good old days. Because of this he held a general aversion towards strangers.

Nick no longer participated in the suspensions. He claimed it was because there were too many outsiders and it was all turning into a giant spectacle. But everyone knew it was because Nick felt too old. He had aching joints and a heavy gut, but worse, he felt a terrible strain upon his heart as if too much exertion would cause it to explode in his chest at any moment. So it made sense that if he could no longer play the game he would enforce the rules. Nick was in training to become a suspension artist, which Trevor supported because it meant good business if they didn't need to pay for an outside technician.

Across the parlor, Nick lay sprawled out on the chaise longue, observing this silent exchange: August fumbling in place while Libby sauntered off. He feigned disinterest, one hand pushing the buttons on his cell phone while the other scratched the mound of belly that crept out from under his shirt. He

thought, "Of course, Trevor invited him. There was no other excuse." If it were up to Nick he'd grab the boy by the nape and toss him outside without a word. But the decision wasn't his and, besides, this gave quite an interesting twist to the morning.

Libby emerged from the office again and glided across the room; her presence alone filled spaces. "I can't find the roster. Does anyone actually work here?"

Nick stared up at her. "I think I'm emotionally wounded," he said. "Deeply. What a curious sensation." Again, she mentioned the roster and Nick sat up, hunched over in a way that turned his broad belly into a compressed barrel. "Veronica left me."

Libby gave him a suspicious look. "Yeah? She leaves you every other week."

"She called me mechanical, that I'm like a wall. That touching me was like feeling a brick wall. What does that even mean?" He gave a pathetic grunt and Libby walked over to him, patting her hand on his thick shoulder. In a large swoop he pulled her into the *V* of his parted legs, leaving only a thin gap between them. "Comfort me," he mockingly whimpered and then caught August's eye. They both looked away.

Libby tilted her head back in an inaudible laugh and plucked off her glasses to wipe the lens on her sleeve. "Tonight we can drink and cry, but right now I need the manifest."

The curtain opened and Trevor emerged with his client, a young man in a brightly colored polo shirt who flexed his bandaged arm like a dowsing rod. With Libby still held over the chaise lounge and Trevor nodding at him, August walked back behind the register as if he'd always worked there. "Whatcha get?" he asked as the receipt printed.

The client was the typical sort: arrogant and vulnerable to flattery. But his smugness faded when he realized the staff was watching them. He could only mumble the word, "Shamrock."

"Neat," August said and everyone laughed. He handed over a complimentary tube of cleansing gel and the client slinked out.

Libby checked her watch and again asked for the roster.

"I thought today would be an intimate gathering," Trevor said. He rubbed the edge of his mustache, sheepishly glancing at his boots. No invitations had been sent. There was no manifest, no paying customers. Usually they had a dozen, enough to pay the technician's fees with plenty left over for a decent profit.

Libby scowled. "How could you? How are we supposed to pay for this? We're so far in the red we're bleeding!"

"He's agreed to do individual rates. It won't cost the store anything. This is more of a favor to me." Trevor slid his arm around her waist. Outside, the occasional car sped by. "We'll be okay," he said. "Today wouldn't make a difference if we sold fifty tickets." And though Libby's head twisted away, he pulled her tighter until she relented, laying her cheek against his shoulder. "Everything will be fine," Trevor said and almost believed it.

A beat-up sedan rolled into the parking lot. The technician entered with a beaming smile that parodied a sitcom father arriving home from work — a strange affectation for a man who pierced body parts for a living. He was muscular, with coarse skin and tiny red fissures staining his cheeks. But he was handsome anyway because of his stature and his politeness. Like a gentleman, he apologized for being late.

"You must be the new guy," the technician said. He stood very close to August, took the boy's hand and squeezed. His flannel shirt gave off a pleasant odor of cologne and musk. "You nervous?" he asked. August shrugged, feeling nothing but compliant and useless until the man released his grip.

Nick took his place behind the counter, retrieving a small lockbox. "Admission time, folks. Checks or cash. Libby, are you paying for two or is he playing voyeur?"

August wiped his sweaty palms off on his jeans. Everyone was looking at him. Libby's head drooped sideways, exposing the muscular lines of her thin neck, as she dangled her checkbook in an accusing manner. Then August felt a flush of anxiety. For a moment his pulse beat with such force that all his arteries twitched in unison. But when Libby closed her checkbook, he blurted, "No, I'm good for this," and she tightened her mouth before scribbling on the check.

"That a boy," Trevor said, pulling a crumpled wad of bills from his oversized wallet.

They retrieved a black duffel bag from behind the counter and walked through the back hallway, passing the dirty unisex bathroom and the employee lockers. The warehouse was a large cavernous space with concrete floors and morose gray walls. Hanging fluorescent lights flickered on, casting a sterile glow. Initially August felt an ominous presence in the warehouse,

Jonathan Harper

but it quickly faded. There was a large red door on the far wall and a metal sink next to a closet. Aside from a few floor mats and storage containers, the warehouse was empty, cold and lacking any clear purpose. The three men had moved on to the storage bins and August turned to his cousin with a perplexed look on his face. "Is this it?" His voice echoed.

"What were you expecting?"

"I don't know. I thought there would be a forklift and cages or a stage?"

"What kind of business do you think I'm running here?" she said and then returned to the front to close up.

From a safe distance he watched the technician set up the equipment. The pulley system went first. Several metal poles fit firmly into small locks on the floor. The poles stood twenty feet tall. They seemed endless, their tops connected by overlapping beams from which several pulleys dangled like evil chandeliers. There was rope and long harnesses with protruding metal loops. It all added to the room's sense of industrial disintegration. They dragged out floor mats under the metal structures and Nick unfolded a large massage table. From the black duffel bag, the technician withdrew the hooks — long, silver, delicate curves — the kind one would take fishing for sea monsters.

"If you want me to use your own, I'll need to sterilize them myself. House rules," the technician said and then beckoned August close, holding out the first hook for the boy to inspect. "This is good quality here. It's sleek enough so it won't feel intrusive, but strong, too. You'd be amazed how much weight they can support."

August felt a looming figure behind him and Nick's hand grasped his shoulder, palpating it like a soft claw. "The newbie goes first," he said.

The technician did not look amused. "He looks ready to faint, if you ask me," and carried the hooks off towards the cleansing station.

"Oh, he's got his eye on you," Nick whispered as he tightened his grip. "Don't get all chickenshit on us." August could feel the man's belly graze his back as if ready to engulf him. He shrank back against it.

"Quit tormenting him, you oaf," Libby said as she returned to the warehouse. She waved her cigarette case and Nick released his grip. They stepped out back to smoke and waited patiently for the technician to finish setting up.

Half a pack later and the group was assembled inside. Trevor agreed to go first and discarded his clothes in a pile until he was left wearing nothing but a pair of nylon shorts. Years of weightlifting had not prevented small love handles from forming at his waist. Both his arms were covered in inked sleeves, a Charybdis whirlpool engulfed a pierced nipple. Tiny rows of blackheads dotted his shoulders — a tuft of hair sprouted above his ass. Without the usual crowd, every footstep echoed through the warehouse. They huddled close, watching as Trevor lay facedown on the massage table and the technician poured cleansing solution and started to knead carefully into the dough of Trevor's back.

"What we're doing here is loosening up the skin from the muscles so we can insert the hooks," the technician said. He had August sitting on a small metal stool with a clear view, Libby standing to the side, her arms wrapped together.

Nick brought over his tray of tools as the technician wiped his hands dry and snapped on surgical gloves. First there was the clamp. It looked like a misshapen wrench, the head a pair of oval jaws that opened to reveal dull little teeth. The center of the clamp was hollow. He attached it to a lump of skin on Trevor's shoulder, exposing a patch of flesh in the center. Next came the piercing needles, followed by the hook. When the clamp lifted, the skin shrank back against Trevor's shoulder blade, revealing the sleek metal that sank in and curved out a few inches below. There was blood, but only a few drops. Five more hooks sat on the table and August, feeling his stomach begin to spasm, sprang off his seat and out through the backdoor.

*W*hen the door closed, it locked automatically behind him. He was in a small alley facing a field of dead grass and the distant train tracks. For a moment he felt ready to vomit or faint but did neither. As the sensation receded, he leaned against the crumpling plaster of the building and stared through the rings of the chain-link fence. Dandelion weeds tangled up in them. He was muttering to himself when Libby came outside, propping the door with her tennis shoe. She placed a cold water bottle against his cheek before she drew a cigarette to her lips, exhaled like a sigh. August buckled at first, but within seconds laid his head against her shoulder while she cradled him in her free arm.

"Why don't we take a drive? There's a good diner about a mile away. We're due for a late brunch."

"I just didn't know it would look like that," he said. The last thing he wanted was her sympathy. "Why didn't you tell me?"

"We did tell you. You asked and we explained and you wanted to be here."

The air was warmer now. He chugged the remainder of the water bottle; cold seeped through his chest. "But I didn't know it was going to be like that." He paused. "Why do you do this?"

Libby's body went rigid. Her cigarette ash hung like a limp dick. Her face had gone vacant as she struggled to find her words. "No one will make you do anything you don't want to do. That's a major rule."

He slumped back. "But I *want* to be made to do something."

Libby snapped her head toward him. She looked disturbed.

"That's not entirely correct," he said and blushed. He didn't know what he wanted.

"Well, you're here now and it's got to be your choice." Libby took another long drag and smirked. "But if you're staying, I'm not doing this topless. I don't want you to see my boobies."

He glared at her. "You do this naked?"

"Trevor does all the time. He's an exhibitionist." She snubbed out the cigarette before adding, "But you can't. That would be way too awkward."

He forced a chuckle and found that he was quite calm. "I'm ready to go back inside if you are."

Libby rose to her feet and pulled him up. But before she let go, she tightened her grip. In that moment, she looked all-knowing and powerful, more so than all the Aunts combined. "Take all the time you need. We'll do whatever you want."

Back inside, Trevor sat up on the massage table, face a little sweaty, six hooks in a line along his upper back. He gave August a wink and moved towards the pulley system. The technician threaded the hooks into a small harness as Trevor stood there calmly. Within a few moments, rope sprouted from Trevor's back, ascending up through the pulleys and dropping out the other side into a serpentine coil. The ropes tightened, the hooks pulled and Trevor's skin stretched into long fleshy pyramids. The technician checked for signs of tearing and as Nick continued to pull Trevor began to rise. There was a moan, a small creak from the metal poles, but otherwise the room remained silent. This was the suicide suspension, the hanging body mimicking one caught in a noose. At first it was a grotesque sight, but then serene. Trevor floated a few feet above the ground, chin pressed firmly against the base of his neck, drifting off in a trance.

"I have to be honest," the technician said, moving closer to August. He kept his voice low. "I'm not feeling confident about you. Do you want to take some more time to think about it?"

August shook his head before Libby could interject. He pulled off his shirt and said, "No, I think we should get this over with." It was not the answer the technician looked for, but it was said in an unwavering voice that could not be refuted.

August shook his head before Libby could interject. "I have to pee," he said and rushed out to the restroom. It took him a long time, forcing out a weak urine stream, his own body fighting against him. As he undressed, his arms trembled but only a little. When he emerged, wearing nothing but a pair of cut-off shorts, his bare feet dashed along the cold concrete and he lay face down on the massage table. "I'm ready," he said and almost meant it.

Trevor dangled in his peripheral vision. As the technician poured the cleansing solution and began to rub him, August felt his erection chafe against the foam padding.

"So tense, so tense. I can feel your heart beating through your back," the technician said quietly. "Tell me when this starts feeling good. I don't want you going around spreading rumors that I'm bad at my job."

But August felt incapable of responding. He was light-headed, well aware of his heartbeat and blood flow. He wanted to float away while the world drifted around him. Libby was there, someplace — he sensed her like a large ball of electricity, pulsing with nervous energy. He could sense Trevor, too, only much higher, dimmed and calm.

"Instead of doing a suicide, I'd like to try a Superman pose. We'll do inserts on your shoulders, lower back, legs and arms. The weight distribution won't be as intense." August barely felt the tingle of the man's finger pressing down on each specified area. "We're going to do this in slow stages. We need to communicate the entire way," the technician assured him.

The hands withdrew, followed by the crass slap of latex.

"I'm going to clamp the skin for the first puncture. I'll wait a few moments before I insert the needle, so if you can't handle the clamp, you need to say something." The voice sounded distilled, as if it were coming from afar. As August continued to drift he became increasingly aware of the emptiness around him until he could see all four corners of the warehouse. From above he caught a glimpse of his body limp on the massage table. He blinked twice and the image faded. Then something scraped against his shoulder blade.

The cold metal teeth of the clamp chewed and required several attempts to grab enough skin. It stung. The technician's hands stroked around the clamp and waited to proceed. "Are you all right?"

"Yes." But whatever had risen submerged, and then came the drop.

"Are you sure?"

"Yes, I'm sure." He told himself, one moment of pain and it'll be over. Like getting an ear pierced or a blood test. Like picking a scab. And then he would stretch, rise and float. There was comfort in shock. Instructions were uttered, but they were incoherently distant. The word "yes" flowed from his mouth.

There was more movement behind him. His vision blurred. Something sharp pushed against his exposed skin in the clamp. "No," August muttered. But the piercing continued and a cold sensation shot into him. "No." The cold spread deep and soon he felt it all over as if a bed of nails slowly pressed upon him. Even his internal organs felt it. A sound of rushing water flooded his ears and his vision was a spectacle of dark spots and dancing lights.

Then August began to scream.

$\mathcal{H}$e awoke sharply to a pungent odor, head twitching away as Libby idled smelling salts under his nose. Her face was calm but her voice stern. "Eyes open. Stay awake," she said as the warehouse slowly came back into focus. The clamp's teeth were gone, his shoulder raw and bruised. Two large hands lay flat against him, enough weight to prevent him from sliding off the table. He took several labored breaths as Libby wiped his brow of sweat with the edge of her shirt, displaying the small creases on her stomach. Instinctively, August peered up and saw the curve of her tit in a black bra, its modest curve shrouded, and he recoiled.

The technician eased his hands and made soothing strokes along the boy's spine. "You're okay, kiddo." Without the pressure, August tried to stand, but his legs wobbled and wouldn't support him. "Not so fast. You relax a bit." Those strong arms scooped him up, cradled him under the arm pits, and August leaned his face against the man's chest and breathed. There was warmth and comfort in the flannel shirt. August imagined burrowing inward, wanted to crawl into the man's chest as if he were a locked garden. Instead, he felt himself being propped in a chair. Trevor's hanging body came into view, his eyes open and alert.

"August, look at me," the technician said. "Can you tell me how many fingers I'm holding up? Can you tell me what day it is?"

The questions were dauntingly stupid. "Three fingers. It's Sunday."

"I promise you, the needle never left the table. I only used the clamp and waited."

August crossed his arms over his chest, tucking one knee up, leaving his other foot firmly planted on the floor.

"No needles, no holes. I promise." The technician gave another reassuring smile.

Libby returned with a soda from the vending machine and August chugged it greedily. He felt humiliated and on the verge of tears as Libby gently rubbed his shoulder.

The technician turned to her. "Did you still want to go today? If so, I'd prefer to wait until your friend is finished." Across the room, Trevor had managed to regain his previous state of peace, though his face looked more determined than lucid. Nick's head remained obscured by one of Trevor's dangling legs.

Libby shook her head. "I think I'll pass."

"Under the circumstances, I'll only charge for one of you."

All of this faded into the recess of his mind as August pinched his chewed fingernails against the skin of his calf. He relished the sharp pain, almost hard enough to break the skin but not quite. It seemed like a trivial sensation. It all did and just beyond, there sat the discarded hooks and the technician, now ready to coach Trevor down.

They rode back in Libby's beat-up van. She insisted the tape deck could only play her David Bowie cassettes, which Nick claimed was her way of torturing him. Because Nick's license had expired he had accepted the offer for a ride and sat up front, letting his fingers create wind fissures out the open window. Trevor sat in the middle bench, exhausted, occasionally singing along to the music in an injured-sounding voice.

August was stretched out on the back bench, body curled as he feigned sleep to avoid conversation. The duffel bag lay just in view under the seat. He thought he'd drift off but the ride unsettled him. The van vibrated as it moved and came to stuttering halts at every red light. It reminded him of that terrible sensation back in Wilford, when he was on the antidepressants. He'd wake up at night with a vague feeling of danger, like an unknown gas leak was slowly asphyxiating everyone. And yet, despite all the paranoia, he felt nothing but indifference to it. Perhaps it was this indifference that had made him so susceptible to his old boss. For a moment he could only see that oafish smile on Chef's plump face and then August couldn't help but remember that first night where Chef had put him on top of the prepping table. He felt utterly disgusted afterward for letting the man fuck him with that piggly little dick greased up in olive oil. The saddest part was August had orgasmed after a mere thirty seconds. He felt it coming out like a sneeze and there was nothing he could do to stop it. "Well, good for you," Chef had grumbled before stomping off. It was unclear why this memory chose to present itself at this particular moment. It made the drive home even more uncomfortable.

$\mathcal{I}$t was late afternoon when they pulled into their side of Sterling. Libby's house backed up to a large brick wall. Years ago a portion of the neighborhood had been demolished and reconstructed into evenly spaced three-story houses now filled with government workers who commuted all the way into D.C. Libby's half of the neighborhood was prospected for great renovations as well, but somewhere along the way the developers lost interest. Now the brick wall remained to keep the communities separate.

"You can feed the Parsons' cats, right?" she asked. August assumed this was her subtle way of telling him the world had returned to normal — that they could all go about their normal routines again. They stood in the kitchen, the duffel bag put away, the two men already in the den raiding the liquor cabinet. Libby uncorked a bottle of Shiraz. "That's okay, right? If you're not going to do it, I just need to know before I end up finishing a bottle." He poured himself a half glass and assured her that he was happy to do so. After all, the Parsons house had a pool and a very tall fence.

But he didn't go to the Parsons' right away. Instead he went upstairs to his bedroom. For years Nick had used it during those stretches of time when he was in between apartments. Now it was decorated pathetically with plastic action figures and taped-up comic strips. An anime poster showed a trio of oval-eyed school girls floating mid-air with whimsical expressions. He set his wine glass on his desk next to a stack of textbooks and thumbed through the pages. As he glanced over highlighted sentences, he listened to the activities downstairs: the muffled conversation through radio music, a toilet flush, Nick loudly reminiscing about eating Veronica's pussy. "Like sweet papaya!" he announced and Libby shrieked. August read a few more lines and, feeling satisfied, closed his notebook and ventured down for more wine.

They all sat in the den, cradling empty glasses. A tin bowl of popcorn sat in the center of the coffee table and the ashtrays already smoldered with little butt gardens. August took slow steps towards the kitchen, trying to look dignified. He wanted them to see him and know he did not require their company.

"There you are," Trevor said. "Why'd you disappear on us?"

"You hungry? We were thinking of ordering Chinese," Libby said.

"No, I don't feel like eating," August replied, even though he was starving. He eyed the popcorn with rapturous want. "Just a little thirsty."

"Well, at least come join us for a bit." Trevor's voice was forcefully energetic. It was astounding how quickly he recovered. "And bring the bottle with you. We're all dry."

August sat on the edge of the stone fireplace, turning his glass in his hand. The conversation shaped itself around the whereabouts of their other friends, people whom August had only met briefly and in small doses. They all had useless art degrees and mundane jobs, illegitimate children and drug stories — even though no one was officially using anymore. Seizing the opportunity, Nick gave a long self-centered speech regarding his recent break-up with Veronica. She had always been selfish and self-destructive. As much as Nick lamented losing her, he appeared to have never liked her in the first place. August glanced at one of the picture frames on the lamp stand. A group of friends posing at a garden party, their faces whitewashed by the flash: Trevor and Libby raised their beers while Nick engulfed an aloof Veronica, who glanced sideways as if spying something beyond the camera. The image filled him with pity for her.

Nick took a long drink and coughed. "I remember one time when she threw a conniption fit over this guy checking out her friend instead of her. She moped about it for an entire day and then wouldn't eat anything all night. When I said I would force something down her throat, she actually cried over it, like I was hurting her."

"It doesn't seem like a fair thing to say when she's not here to defend herself," August said and immediately regretted it.

"Defend herself? She got off on being humiliated." Nick downed the remainder of his drink. "It was just like you and Duncan. Remember him?" August did remember Duncan, the filmmaker with bad teeth who gave excellent head. They'd met his first week in town and their affair had ended

Jonathan Harper

badly. "He told me he still has those pictures he took of you and jerks off to them, the sentimental bastard."

"Nick, please. I don't need these mental images," Libby said.

"Why not? It's the same thing. These kids beg to be used and abused and then run off crying at the last possible moment."

Trevor leaped from his spot on the couch and retrieved the Risk board out from its hiding place in the cupboard. Everyone moaned.

"Come on! I feel like I can take over the world right now." He set up the board and placed the cards in a large lopsided pile. "I'll even let you be purple," he said and tossed one of the plastic containers of miniature armies to August, who rolled his eyes.

"Take a seat, little man," Nick said to him. "One complaint and I'll wipe you off the face of the earth." The disturbing, blank quality of his eyes dissipated and refocused. They flickered as if they were masterminding deep calculations. August thought he imagined it. He did not.

They settled into the board game. Besides the slight distance he felt between them, August was amazed how ordinary they all behaved. His life had not been disarrayed by the events of the afternoon. More drinks were consumed, they argued briefly over the music. Trevor was forceful with his affection, grabbing August's knee or trying to twist his nipple when he rolled the dice. Unfortunately, August had terrible strategy and spread himself too thin over Europe, which made for an early elimination.

"Surrender and go fill up wine," Libby shrieked, waving a finger. With a final dice roll, she plucked up the last purple army piece from Iceland and was the new ruler of Europe. August cursed, grabbed the two wine glasses and stomped back to the kitchen. In a hushed voice, someone called him a sore loser.

One of the glasses fell into the sink and shattered. It was a cheap little goblet, brightly painted with earthy browns and reds, now in shards that sat dangerously close to the drain. He stood there staring at them for what felt like a long time until Nick sauntered in with his glass empty. "I'm dead. Africa does not love me and your cousin's a fiend," he slurred. "I hear there's Wild Turkey in here."

August motioned to the top of the fridge to the unopened bottles and turned back to fish out a glass shard. Then Nick impulsively slapped him on the ass with a swift open-palm strike. "I said get me my Wild Turkey," he ordered as August yelped. Nick stood there, beaming with satisfaction as Au-

$\mathcal{N}$ATURE

gust retrieved the bottle, twisted off the cap and poured it into Nick's empty glass. "Want some?" he asked as he dangled the glass by its rim, the sweat of the ice almost making it slip from his fingers. "Take a sip," Nick ordered.

August narrowed his eyes at the brown liquor, worried he'd gag, but did as he was told. It seared his throat as it went down.

"Good boy," Nick said. And then he reached around and encased one of August's ass cheeks in his hand and squeezed: soft, pudgy, like Veronica's breasts. The boy just stood there, the same confused stupid look on his face that Nick had watched for months. "It's okay. We all need to play a role," Nick said as his voice drifted into some private thought.

"Where the hell is my wine?" Libby called.

"Hold your horses, vile woman! I'm giving your cousin a stiffy." Nick laughed.

The confusion lifted in an angry steam cloud and August pushed Nick back. It had the same effect of slamming against a concrete wall, but Nick stepped away as Libby sauntered in, peering at both of them.

"What's going on?"

"Nothing." August covered his erection with his arm.

Libby swayed a little in place, but otherwise appeared sober. "Well, come back in here. This is going to be the shortest game ever. He's got me on the run." Trevor hollered from the den as she grabbed her glass, unmindful of the one that had shattered, and waltzed back out with an extra bottle. "Nick, stop being a brute or I'll smack you. August, don't you dare get drunk until you've gone to the Parsons."

The keys sat out on the edge of the counter top. They called to August, a reminder that he still had a responsibility: he should pick them up and walk out into the evening. Across the room, Nick slumped in a chair at the dinette, his fingers twisting a wayward hair from his sideburns. Both Nick and the keys beckoned. If he did leave now, whatever this moment represented would remain unfinished and probably not repeat itself.

"So what now?" he asked.

The brute licked his lips and gave a combative look, leaned back in the chair and undid the buttons of his shorts. He tugged the waistband of his briefs low enough to reveal his his busy pubes, his firecrotch, sprouting below his belly. There was nothing serious about it, no different than Trevor flashing his genitals for a reckless laugh. Only this time August didn't feel

scandalized. Instead he felt challenged, approached Nick slowly with a hand on his hip and asked, "Is that all?"

Nick smiled, squeezed his tongue between his teeth. He slid the waistband down further. His penis was sweaty and coiled in the briefs. Then he grabbed the boy's arm and pulled him down to meet it. What August didn't know, what he could never know, was that Nick was thinking of Veronica. She now existed in that mental kaleidoscope of past love affairs and conquests: her eyes drooping sadly as he bound her hands behind her back, as he placed her on all fours and slapped her exposed vagina. He languished in this memory and then shut it off with one last farewell. A mouth is a mouth.

August knelt before him, at first reluctant, but then fell into the old habit. There was music and laughter coming from the den. Tom Petty sang, dice rolled and Libby called Trevor an asshole. August could hear everything as he worked his mouth. He tasted sweat and grime and felt belly hairs brush against his forehead. Nick's hand dug underneath the collar of August's shirt, his chewed fingernails scratched at the tender spot on the boy's shoulder blade. Then August felt Nick's cock bury deep into his mouth. A push, a shove, a grunt. "Don't fight it," Nick muttered in repetition as warm liquid shot into the warm throat. August fought his way up out of the man's grasp and spit the rest out into the sink.

Nick let out a heavy breath as he pulled up his briefs; the shape of his cock deflated and left a small dark spot on his shorts. "Here, drink this," and Nick handed over the glass with the remaining swallows of bourbon left, which August drank with a grimace. Again, Nick laughed, rose and walked back out to the den where Trevor was undoubtedly taking over the world.

"He may be a pussy at times, but damn he's got a mouth like a Hoover," Nick said.

"Jesus Christ, shut the fuck up, you pig." Libby rushed back into the kitchen, her eyebrows raised in a pointed arch. She had trouble finding her center of balance with a wine-induced look of disorientation. "Where's your glass?" she asked, motioning to the bottle of Shiraz.

August stayed quiet at first, face furrowed as he watched his foot tap against alternate tiles. "I forgot to go feed the cats," he said.

*I*t was only a ten-minute walk past the barriers that separated the neighborhoods. August had only seen the Parsons' home once before, on another cat feeding expedition. He knew Mrs. Parsons was a homemaker and a mother of two, that she attended Libby's yoga class and occasionally invited her over for coffee. The woman probably loved having a younger friend who consorted with artsy types.

The house contained a large foyer with an Oriental rug and a floating bronze chandelier. It reminded August of his grandmother's home, larger but equally ornate. There were expensive displays of artwork and antique furniture everywhere. The cats, two sleek Siamese, encircled his feet, screeching for dinner with long dramatic howls. He split a can of tuna-flavored mush into the silver bowls, changed the litter box and emptied the trash.

The real reward for his efforts was the pool out back, blocked from view by the topiary and the privacy fence. It was late and dark. The pool lights were not on and a light fog hovered above the water. August found the children's gear in the laundry room, inflated the water wings and carried them out in bundles. He undressed, the cats spying through the blinds. "Don't tattle on me," he said and then slipped the water wings into rows on each leg and arm.

The pool shocked him with coldness. It was still too early in the season to swim, but his body adjusted slowly. He floated on his back, bringing himself to perfect stillness. Time moved very slowly in the dark. There was much left to do: finish his classes at the tech school, earn a living, eventually find his own place. His shoulder blade still felt tender, a small ache but no pain. It felt like a subtle tapping, a reminder that he'd been daydreaming way too long. This is what it must feel like: the weightless sensation, the quiet drifting, only a sharp, subtle reminder that the ground was still nearby.

The Cake is a Lie

*Y*ou wouldn't have recognized me last summer.

Last summer I was twenty-nine and about thirty pounds lighter. Back then I was the walking breathing definition of mediocrity, with a baby face and freckles that did me no justice. I had no big plans, no dramatics and a part-time job at a bakery down the road. Then the housing bubble burst and foreclosure signs started sprouting up like sad little monuments all over the neighborhood. I kept thinking, if I hadn't squandered most of my money on culinary school, I could swoop in and purchase a small house for a fraction of its value. Then I'd wait out the markets, sell it for a fortune and become a serious real estate mogul. As it was I never ventured any further than my apartment balcony. I sat outside for hours, smoking Parliaments and imagining another wad of cash appearing in my pockets and the many ways to spend it.

The point is, I was content meandering through life and I had dependable stoic Louis to rely on. He was fifty-four and well established with a cushy government job at the National Archives. We had managed three pleasant years together. It was a good relationship, no worse than any other. Since we survived that tedious first year (when he vied for the attention of a younger man and I had to prove my maturity to an older one), I found that I was well suited for domestic life in the suburbs. I wasn't pretty or successful enough for the in-crowds of D.C., nor was I intelligent enough to talk politics with these men who wore business suits more expensive than my rent. I figured all I needed out of life was my part-time job, a balcony herb garden and a clean apartment with a spare room for our sex sling, which Louis and I used on occasion.

When Louis started looking at the foreclosures, I felt the urge to be productive as well. I was a pastry chef by trade and fell into a lucid fantasy of owning my own shop. Soon it was all I could think about — what else was there for me to do? Every night I stayed up late in the kitchenette, trying to invent a personal spin on my recipes. I'd find myself issuing instructions to a make-believe staff or greeting some imaginary client. This was for practice and inspiration and because I was lonely. It would be well after midnight when I pulled the latest concoction out of the oven. Then Louis would call out, "Frankie, come to bed." I always obeyed, crawled under the sheets, gently brushed my knuckles against his spine and thought, *daddy*. Like son.

My best friend, Maria, didn't approve of me buying a house with Louis. She thought him too old and stodgy and because of him I was turning into a recluse. "If you do this, you'll turn into his little housewife forever." This was the sort of thing you can say when you've known someone for years and have seen them at their worst. Back in college, we had that messy sort of friendship, full of fights and shared lovers — the kind of past you sometimes want to distance yourself from but can't. I won't lie to you, she had her shit together long before I did. Maria had a banking career and bought a condo right outside the city. I was lucky she still bothered to drive half an hour out of the city just so we could drink our lunch and reminisce about our old affairs.

I don't know what instigated her vendetta against Louis. She acted like she wanted me single and drifting, even when she announced her own engagement to a nice man whom I liked but did not consider marriage material. He was too young, for starters, and did not share Maria's business savvy or work ethic. They didn't even live together. Despite my concerns, her wedding cake became my first solo commission. With all my free time, I practiced stacking tiers of yellow cake and molding snapdragon flowers out of gum paste. But with a friendship like ours, how could we not end up butting heads over each other's decisions? It turned into our massive fight, where years' worth of unresolved issues resurfaced. Even though I wasn't sorry, the mere mention of her name depressed me. I lost the commission and had to find a new best friend. On the rare occasion I turned to Louis for sympathy, he'd pat my shoulder in a casual way. "Don't complain to me. I never liked her in the first place."

ℋow does one make the transition from houseboy to small business owner? To start, fall into helping hands. Then, have enough money in the bank for them to trust you with a loan. I had both: Louis with his meticulous eye for business plans and my own modest chunk of money left over from my inheritance. My parents were long dead, thank goodness, my mother to kidney failure and my father to a heart attack two months after. When they died I cashed in their insurance policies, sold their house, and for the first time savored the taste of wealth. I paid off my college debts, went to

culinary school and, while sheltered under Louis's wing, still had enough left over to start a project.

When I told Louis I wanted to open a little café in our neighborhood, he started planning the next day. We were a quiet task-driven household. If there wasn't business to discuss, or if I didn't talk to myself or leave the television on, the apartment rang with an unbearable silence. Two days could go by like this and then he'd look up from the housing section of the newspaper and say things like, "I'm okay with you doing what you like, but you need to be doing more."

But the banks were reluctant to lend money, even with Louis's intervention. The words "market crash" and "recession" were spiked into our heads by a dozen consultants. "This is not the time," they'd say. But what else could we do? Sit around moping over a bad economy? I would only be stressing over an impossible reconciliation with Maria. We kept looking, pushing against the bankers, and finally everything worked out. We got our house and my café opened for business and I even found a new best friend. He was the easiest. We met him at the swimming pool.

Our rental was in a complex of eighteen garden apartment buildings lined up in two semicircles. The pool sat bull's eye. Despite the plague of heatwaves, so grueling that members of the elderly walking group dropped dead every other week, the pool was often deserted. The only other people there were the Czech lifeguard (whose trunks were always just revealing enough to entice) and the obese Betty Boop who doggie-paddled slowly through the water. Sometimes there was the overly-affectionate couple we'd nicknamed "Thing One" and "Thing Two," but they never stayed out long. It was peaceful enough for Louis to swim his laps while I read a copy of *Entrepreneurship for Beginners*. I would poke through it, annoyed, as I read about the necessity of market research without any instruction on how to conduct it.

If I had not met Briar, last summer might have drifted by in a slow, predictable fashion until I too quit going to the pool at all. When he was there he was solitary, drifting in and out of the backdrop. Briar was more Maria's type than mine: skinny, pigeon-faced, his hair dyed black. He liked comic books and getting stoned. This is the part where I'm supposed to provide some anecdote on how we met to foreshadow his importance. I could give a humorous account of Briar diving into the pool and losing his swimsuit, or that

I caught him giving Louis that creepy-eyed *come-hither* look, even if neither of these things happened. At the outset, he blended in with the countless residents in Tyson's Glen and very few of them ever left an impression. For a year I kept bumping into my neighbor at the mailbox without so much as a cordial hello. So why Briar stood out amongst them, I have no idea. But once I noticed him, I couldn't *help* but notice him, the same way you notice your partner arriving home late at night, smelling of bar soap and cologne — and you can't stop analyzing their every gesture.

Together he and I sat on the edge of the pool, smoking too many Parliaments, and talked about our aspirations. He was waiting for his abstract paintings to get discovered. I told him about my future bakery. We made self-deprecating jokes about the pitiful state of our lives, the fact that we were not prodigies and patience had not worked in our favor. And when Louis joined us, dripping wet and reeking of chlorine, Briar shifted into quiet self-consciousness, picking at his nails until it was time to go.

Whenever I mentioned Briar's name, I could sense Louis tense up. He always responded to my ramblings with head nods and groans, but this was different. I'd take the trash out to the dumpsters and return an hour later, smelling of smoke. Louis would stomp into the next room, knowing who I'd run into. To him, home was a sacred place of solace. We never had visitors. Interaction was something that happened in the outside world and he did not want me bringing it in.

Once I suggested we go to Briar's apartment. "He's showing off his paintings to a few people and he'd like us both to come. We're the only neighbors he talks to," I said.

Louis grumbled something over the MLS forms his real estate agent had sent him. "We can't go. There's too much going on," he replied, which wasn't true. I casually brought up the party every other day, mentioned how I had already volunteered to bring food and how excited I was to see the artwork until Louis finally relented. "You go and play with your little friends," he said, acting like it was a great sacrifice.

$\mathcal{I}$ brought over two trays of ladyfingers and little madeleines. Briar lived across the complex in one of the rent-controlled efficiencies. It was in a marvelous state of decay, smelling of weed and rotten fruit. Metal shelving units lined the walls, each overstuffed with dripping paint canisters, brushes, books and knick-knacks. A sad futon bed was shoved in the corner.

There was no natural light. His friends, all equally young and important, sat in a cluster, playing a video game. They offered me a joint without introducing themselves. And for a moment I felt nostalgic for the chaos of the old college dorm rooms where, years ago, Maria and I had first met.

I looked hard into Briar's paintings: big amorphic blobs of color with little human figures sketched roughly into the middle. "They're quite scary, aren't they?" I said and noticed his eyebrow arch upward. "The colors are so dark and there's so much texture. I prefer earth tones mostly, but these are really intense. Were you in art school? No? Well, I think they're brilliant, really I do."

Echoes of agreement came from around the apartment and Briar gave an exasperated smile. "I'm already bored with them. I want to try something new, something post-modern," he said.

"Isn't everything post-modern at this point?" I asked and no one laughed.

But I haven't mentioned the girlfriend, even though she had been there the entire time. Melissa was a busty woman in her late twenties with olive skin and dark hair that cascaded down her back. Stuck in this shabby apartment, she appeared as a glimmering diamond among dingy glass ornaments. Sequestered on the futon, she took long mournful drags off her joint, occasionally letting out a delicate cough. I thought to myself, what an odd couple, the artist and the statue, and then thought how she could be lumped into the same category as Louis: caring and aloof, perhaps not able to return affection in public.

I wanted to like her but I didn't. Melissa was the kind of woman who hid her blunt rudeness behind a self-conscious demeanor. She habitually cut Briar off mid-sentence and recoiled from his friends. Even at the swimming pool, she lounged on her chair like an Egyptian princess and complained. We talked too much for her tastes. It was always too hot and the water was too cold and why couldn't we go to a restaurant like normal people? I'm not sure why she tolerated me, when she openly despised everyone else. Perhaps she thought we had a commonality. When you are older, successful and vaguely pretty, you might assume others will naturally follow your lead. Personally, I have little patience for those who lose touch with the frivolous joys of their younger selves and therefore expect others to do the same.

After two beers and a round on Briar's plastic dart board, she pulled me aside for a little chat. "Stop flattering him so much," Melissa said. "You're setting up unrealistic expectations." This came from a woman who probably filled her own house with the sterile mass-produced art from a department store's sale aisle. She told me, "I've heard about your great business plans. I hope you know it takes more than a few baking skills to actually run a café." She criticized my trays of goodies, loudly said that my ladyfingers were hard enough to crack her teeth.

Then she ate half of them.

Briar walked me to the door. "See you at the pool," he slurred. "Give my regards to Louis."

"Yes, where is Louis? Why didn't he come along?" Melissa asked.

I watched Louis through the sluggish lens of a half bottle of wine. His laptop was open to a real estate website. Before we met he owned a restored row house near Capitol Hill with his previous lover, and when their relationship soured they rushed to sell. It should have made them rich; it set the standard.

"What about this one? It's got a sunroom." He pointed to his computer screen.

"The kitchen looks awful," I said.

"Here's a nice one. Lots of space and everything's updated." I took one glance at the pictures and said the yard was too big. I wouldn't mow it. "You're not even trying," he snapped.

I sighed indulgently and stared into the laptop, clicking on icons at random. Here was a tiny rambler that looked pleasant enough and well within our price range. The listing described an open floor plan and a gourmet kitchen. The yard was small and manageable. "I like this one," I said and Louis called his agent to arrange a viewing.

We drove through town. Over the past three years, several mixed-use buildings had been erected along Broad Street: luxury condominiums with long storefronts on street level. Most of them were still empty. The major signs of life came from the new brewery and Panera Bread. I rolled my eyes at the competition.

Up close, the rambler was a morose box-cut house with overgrown grass; it slouched in comparison to its neighbors. Waiting for us was the contemptuous Mr. Spencer, our real estate agent. I greatly disliked him and his snobby mannerisms, the fact that he never spoke to me directly. He gave the impression of the type of man who slinks away from the Annual Republican Picnic

to score a blowjob in the men's room at Macy's. He led us inside with a quick reminder that he was in a hurry.

"You see," Louis said. "Your dream kitchen right here. You could run your own catering company out of this."

Mr. Spencer nodded with disinterest. "This room over here is an addition. It cuts into the backyard, but it makes a good TV room or an office." As we continued our tour, I grew more and more disconnected. I liked our apartment and our weekly routine.

"Upstairs needs work," he continued. "You'll have to use your imagination." He pointed out the master bedroom, a modest size with a tiny bathroom that made Louis frown. Dual wires poked out from the ceiling where a fan had been. Many foreclosures were vandalized by the previous owners. We had seen smashed cabinets, unhinged doors and walls stained with the smell of urine. This was not bad. "Let's continue over here, please. I think this bedroom would be perfect for your son."

Son? I thought. Was he serious? Louis frowned again.

"Well, Frankie, is this room big enough for you?" Mr. Spencer asked me. His smile looked painful and fake. Out of spite, I resigned myself to dislike the rambler.

"It might make a good guestroom," I said and walked out of the room.

Louis was in a foul mood on the ride home. He clutched the steering wheel as if it was a weapon. Out of habit, I started to call Maria, but thought better of it, wondering how long this awkward habit would persist, or if we'd ever work out our problems.

"Do I really look that young?" I asked.

"No. He was insulting me," Louis said.

"Oh," I said, and we retreated back into our usual silence.

At home, Louis huddled in front of his computer and grumbled under his breath. I went into the kitchenette for my nightly baking practice. I melted butter in a fondue pot and mixed eggs, flour, sugar and a few drops of vanilla. A strange feeling lingered within me: an unexplainable yet underwhelming sense of disappointment. Only while I worked did it fade. I didn't even notice Louis standing next to me until I slapped his finger away from the batter.

"Wanna fool around?" he asked.

"Always. But not now."

I filled the madeleine plaque and put it in the oven and soon the whole apartment was filled with a warm aroma. I started to give Louis a blowjob but when the timer went off I left him unfinished in front of the television. The madeleines looked perfect and for a moment, I had this contented image of me placing them on a serving tray in front of a fan of customers. Then I thought of Melissa — *if only she could see me now.*

The Fourth of July came and went and the teenagers were pillaging the local fireworks stand, buying everything on clearance. We could hear them at night, congregated in the high school parking lot, setting off firecrackers and spinners. Then came a series of thunderstorms and this broke up our cozy routine. For two weeks straight there was nothing but rain. Louis put his house hunt on hold and we couldn't even go to the pool, but at least the teenagers had a temporary ceasefire. With nothing better to do, I took extra shifts at the bakery. I'd return home exhausted and sweaty, checked real estate ads before de-cluttering the apartment. Dinner was served when Louis arrived back from work, pan-seared fish or chicken cutlets, sides of roasted vegetable platters, stuffed peppers, couscous salads and anything else I could slap together. Then we'd sit in front of a movie with him hunched over his plate like a feral animal. Why I remember this time as such a content one, I don't know. But it was.

I did not expect Briar to show up on my doorstep, uninvited and dripping wet and a little drunk. It was early afternoon, the lights flickering from the storms. After a tiring morning shift, I'd been half-asleep and half-naked on the couch, listening to the sound of rain pelting against the balcony. His knocking was as loud as thunder and yanked me out of a vague dream. Sluggishly, I answered the door in a bathrobe and briefs, found him there, his eyes glazed over. I pulled my robe tighter. I had been masturbating earlier and worried there might be a stain.

"Melissa and I had a fight and I want to punch someone right now."

In the time it took me to get dressed he had kicked off his muddy shoes in the vestibule and was pulling out bottles from Louis's wine fridge. He smelled good, tart.

"She told me I had no ambition," he said and that their argument had escalated into a shitstorm. He insisted he did have ambition, just not flowing in the direction she wanted. He called her a bitch and stomped out, leaving her in the apartment. She was probably still there destroying everything. I did not have much sympathy for her. Younger lovers come with a price. We require patience and guidance. We think we have all the time in the world.

Jonathan Harper

"Face it. You're dating an older woman. If you don't fit into her long-term plans, then you're wasting her time." I was trying to be diplomatic.

"Well, what are your long-term plans?" he asked.

"I don't know. I'm not an older woman."

I served us more drinks as he glanced through the mounds of paperwork on the dining table, all my business plans and loan applications. At the bookshelf, he inspected a picture of my parents and then took a harder look at a photo of me and Maria in a sushi bar, both of us posed with our chopsticks. "She's beautiful in this one," he said. In the kitchenette, I made little olive and mushroom quiches in a cupcake tin. I poured more drinks, terribly aware I would throw up later. Briar kept asking the time, suggesting he should leave before Louis got home. We drank more and moved to the couch, his hand falling on my knee and rubbing it gently.

"Oh, we're doing that," I said.

He laughed. "Doing what?"

I don't know why I took him to the back bedroom. My entire body moved on autopilot, cradling my wine glass, knowing I was too drunk to be trusted. Part of me simply wanted to shock him, to prove there was something edgy behind my placid existence. Briar stared with great interest at the sex sling, the metal frame canopy that suspended the leather hammock. The windows were blocked with heavy drapes, a tarp laid out over the carpet; the room smelled of sex.

Briar's laugh was loud and cautious. *Freaky*, he called it.

I spilled a few drops of wine over my trembling hand. The other brushed against his hip. And though his body tightened, he gave no other hints whether I should retreat or proceed. I know now that if I had withdrawn my hand and acted as if I had played a magnificent joke, that he would have relished being the punch line. But I didn't; my fingers traced inward, grazing the hard bone of his hip and deeper still, twisting under the waistband of his pants and into the bush of pubic hair, hoping to feel his hard-on. And that was where I lost him.

Briar pulled away. "No," he said. He stumbled backward, clutching his glass so hard it I worried it would shatter. My stomach plummeted. It had happened so fast that I wondered if I was still sleeping on the couch, listening to the storm, caught in a soured dream. Briar stood there, wobbly at first, and then brusquely walked away. The quiches started to smoke in the oven. He fumbled with his shoes, not bothering to tie the laces, not looking up once. And then he was gone. A nagging swirl in my gut told me something hideous had occurred.

*E*ven when the storms passed, I refused to go to the pool. I only went out for my work shifts and promptly returned to hide in the apartment. Louis continued to regard me with amiable disinterest. He hinted once or twice at the untouched financial documents that still needed signatures. He forged on with the house hunt alone. More often than not I felt a strange mix of contempt and desire for him. For a while, I felt like I was living with a stranger, us not talking, not making eye contact, his subtle complaints.

This was last summer and I was a different sort of creature then: lethargic, sunburnt and prone to sudden unexplainable mood swings. I have done my best to paint myself in a fair but accurate light. Perhaps I have watered myself down, the worst thing you can do with top-shelf liquor, to make myself seem passive and delicate. I am anything but that. I left out the part where I started openly feuding with Melissa, encouraging Briar to pass up a job promotion to focus on his art, and stressed hidden meanings behind every disagreement. She even confronted me, dressed up in her silk dress and heels, explaining that she saw the gleam in my eyes for her boyfriend. It became my duty to expose her as the kind of woman who blurred the lines between being protective and jealous, the way she hovered too close like a shield, how she tried to rewrite all of our dialogues.

I realize now that I've made Louis seem nothing but dodgy and selfish. But he did bother to ask about my day and insisted I go with him to more open houses or to the pool. Gifts would appear on the dining table, a folded shirt or a new CD. He even asked if I had heard from Maria. Sometimes a man's reserved quiet stands for his greatest affections and I worry that I've down-played his tenderness all this time. I resumed cooking our dinners of stewed shrimp and mango chutney. He helped get my business permits approved. We fucked in the sex sling. The events of that afternoon with Briar, which seemed like an eternity ago, never surfaced to haunt me.

One day, as if sensing a slight relapse into my previous depression, Louis said, "Cheer up, Frankie. We're going to get settled soon enough and everything will turn out fine."

I assumed he meant my café. Instead, this was Louis's way of announcing he'd closed on a house, a little Cape Cod with a large slate-stoned fireplace and a galley kitchen that was not extravagant but more than suitable for my

needs. We moved in at the beginning of September, after the long arduous process of packing up the apartment and moving my parents' best furniture out of storage. A celebration took place at a bar downtown, where friends from every nook and cranny of Louis's old life resurfaced. They wished us well and bought me more drinks than I could ever finish. We drove home with an entire terrarium's worth of little potted plants they brought as gifts. We received a card with a pastel drawing of a castle by the sea, the word "Congratulations" written in Maria's telltale cursive.

Even the bakery made a contribution. My boss, a jovial woman pushing seventy, spent an entire morning perusing our catalogue for the perfect housewarming gift. What we decided on wasn't as extravagant as the wedding cake I mentioned at the beginning of this story. Instead, we settled on a modest groom's cake with a ganache coating the color of tar. I wrote our names on top with the icing gun.

Our new house was still cluttered with unpacked boxes. There were walls to repaint and a toilet that didn't flush properly, but I thought it was a lovely home, though too large and gaudy for just the two of us. (The garden out back took a while to resurrect, but in the end it rivaled Eden.) I laid a crumpled linen runner over the dining table, fished out the glass server and two dessert plates from my mother's good china. Louis came home, still too quiet and aloof for my tastes, but beaming with pride. And there waiting for him was my cake glistening under the lamp light. His eyes filled with gluttony.

"Oh, we can't eat all this. What a wicked thing to do," he said and patted his belly.

"Go on," I told him. "I've been waiting all day."

Instead, Louis changed into his gym clothes as if to prove a point. As much as I pouted, he turned his attention to stocking the bookcase in the den and hanging picture wires. I finally cut myself a slice and wandered in after him, forking a healthy bite. "It doesn't taste as good when you're eating by yourself," I said. So he surrendered and ate a sliver, warning me the remainder would be thrown out in the morning.

$\mathscr{A}$ year later when Briar resurfaced, looking haggard and much sadder than I remembered, I was filled with fondness for him, and despair and concern — and perhaps a little apprehension. He had come in with the haughtiness of an old friend expecting a favor, still dressed in the same shabby clothes I remembered. And here I was, standing in my own café,

$\mathscr{T}$HE CAKE IS A LIE

a full-bodied entrepreneur with write-ups from the local newspaper and a staff of well-groomed young people to handle the customers. I had grown soft with a newly pronounced belly-bulge, my face healthy and hair already streaked with a few lines of gray.

"Just so you know, we close in half an hour," I overheard the cashier tell him as he walked in. She was a local college student, one of the perkiest young ladies I'd ever met, who fluttered about like an anime character. Briar sat at the pedestal table by the bay window, overlooking the afternoon traffic along Broad Street, across from the tuxedo rental and the bank, and I approached, balancing his coffee on a tray.

"You look so thin," I told him, because he did. There was an unhealthy quality to him, the kind brought on by too much drink and smoke. I wondered when was the last time he'd eaten a full meal.

Briar ignored my comment. "This place looks great," he said. "You actually did it. Not a lot of people can say that."

He was looking at the art posters I had haphazardly hung around the store. They were large art deco prints: Parisian cafés, jazz musicians and a devil guarding a bottle of champagne, all of which I purchased wholesale. I could tell he didn't like them. His brow became increasingly furrowed as he methodically tapped his foot across the toffee-colored floor tiles. But he didn't say so. Instead, he asked if I still spoke to Maria. I nodded, said we had patched things up and she was even getting along with Louis in a way she never had before. We wandered into other topics. He was painting portraits now and had taken a low-impact job with a hotel to pay the bills. There was pride in his voice, more so about what he was working on than what he had achieved.

"Do you ever promote local artists? Lots of coffee shops do. When I get the next batch done, maybe I could try selling them here," he said. I shrugged and thought "no" because I had already seen the quality of his art.

*C*an I tell you that Briar was not an artist?

He was, in fact, a decent guitar player and a mediocre singer whose real name was Brandon. Briar was the stage name, possessing an earthy grungy sound that was distinct, so it stuck. I wrote him in as a painter because I know practically nothing about art and culture, but I love artists, or at least the idea of them. Plus, if I had told you that he was really a musician, then

the circumstances of how we met would have drastically changed, and that might have conveyed a different impression.

Here's how we actually met: Maria and I saw his band play at the Dogwood Tavern. The more beer we drank, the more fantastic they sounded. She had a penchant for dangerous hipster boys in trouble, just like I had my daddy fetish, and she was determined to seduce Briar and make him her boyfriend.

And since I've gone this far, then I'll reveal my biggest deception. Maria and Melissa were actually the same person. Compartmentalizing her made it easier for me to parse out the most complicated relationship of my life. I let Maria stay the absent best friend and Melissa became the overbearing girl-friend who was easy to despise. It wasn't a simple argument that separated us. It was dueling for the attention of a young musician, it was a decade of knowing each other's faults, it was realizing we were turning thirty and had not yet grown into the adult lives we felt we were owed. At times I didn't like her attitude or her fancy new job at the mortgage company. She didn't approve of my relationship with Louis and claimed I was an emotional and financial sponge, which made me question her motives for taking on Briar as her man-child/lover/project/slave.

The loss of that friendship, though it seemed justifiable at the time, carried the weight of a divorce. Maria had been my only friend to attend both of my parents' funerals and who still bothered to keep in touch even as I fell into a secluded suburban way. I grieved over our separation and I was so angry and bitter that I wished harm upon her. Not physical harm, but an emotional tumor that would gnaw at her insides a little more each day. When someone knows you for so long, they know how to manipulate the details. And it was easy for me to fake the desired apology, easy to agree that engagements can happen overnight, easy to invite over a younger boyfriend, one I had grown quite fond of, and under the guise of drunken honesty, convince him that engagements can be broken. What I did not expect was for him to want me as much as he wanted Maria.

That afternoon, in the apartment, when I said Briar rebuffed me? He didn't. The sex was thrilling and awkward, and complicated by too much drink. When we finished, he scurried out and I was left with the hollow feel-ing of guilt and grief, knowing that I had ruined one long-term friendship and jeopardized a new one.

Louis and I complemented each other well enough, all things considered, except that Maria hated him and was convinced he was cheating on me. But she knew our back story and, while she never approved, she had learned to accept it. When I first met Louis, he was partnered with a nice man his own age and I was meant to be a casual one-night fling. And because of the ageist politics of queer D.C., it was getting harder to bring home young, eager men for a tryst. I was the only one who kept coming back, invited first by both of them and then only by Louis. He didn't like sharing me, he said, which sounded ridiculous and very flattering. Before our affair could run its course, Louis and his partner grew sour towards each other. Technically, the partner owned the house, so we moved into the suburbs and for three years I lived with a man who proved no more faithful than an itchy trigger finger. The understanding was that I could have other friends if I liked and that a good boyfriend should share whatever he found. When Louis finally bought the house, he was reluctant to include me as a joint owner on the mortgage. But I suppose he did love me enough and knew that I needed security, considering my fragile state. Our compromise was that I be named as the beneficiary, hence why I avoided his friends and their awful jeers.

Yes, my parents were dead and there were life insurance policies and an expensive house to sell. But there were also taxes, debts and a brother in California with whom I've never shared so much as a pleasant conversation. Of course he swooped in and took command in closing down our parents' estate and my cut was suspiciously small. But I had no access to the paperwork and no clear mind to understand it. I took what I could get and had enough to start culinary school but dropped out after the first semester. Everything I knew was learned from the bakery and my bleeding-heart boss, who acted like a grandmother to anyone who wanted it. When she decided to sell it was much easier to liquidate my small savings and combine that with a loan than it would have been to build up a business from scratch. I am left with the deep-seated ambiguity of the self-made and the financially assisted. And though I have traded my weekends and free time for endless work weeks and weight gain, I have a profession that keeps my mind occupied and an investment to grow and eventually sell off to the next highest bidder. Every Monday I close up shop for a much needed breather and take a fresh pack of cigarettes out to my lovely garden and keep with the old tradition of imagining another inheritance and another future.

I have learned how to reinvent the past.

I knew Briar was in trouble the moment I met him. There was no present visible danger, but it was the kind of trouble you'd expect for a young man

with no life experience and a modest amount of talent, someone who could only daydream with professional execution. I wanted Briar. I wanted to be Briar. All I ever wanted was to be adored and cared for. There was this silly little fantasy I use to play in my head over and over: we all owned a nice house, where Louis was in charge, Maria and Briar had separate bedrooms down the hall and every night they were seated around a large harvest table waiting for me to serve them dinner.

$\mathcal{M}$y cashier hovered politely until I told her to go home; I'd close up myself. Briar had no intention of leaving. He acted like he wanted this afternoon to stretch out forever. I brought him a cold soup and sandwich, free of charge of course. Something for an old friend, I told him and instantly his face brightened. Even if our conversation was flighty, he was still eager to impress me with talk of his work and romantic exploits. I let out a few haughty laughs and remembered the lies I use to tell for a bit of attention.

I thought of my old self from a year ago, that morose creature, and how I left him buried in that old apartment, a compact cell of carpet and drywall. And now I bake wedding cakes and whistle to the sound of my espresso machine. Every day a dozen neighbors come to my doorstep to regale me with local gossip. I have a new writer friend who sits in the corner every weekend and types into her computer, claiming I'm a character in her latest novel. And when the little league comes in, the boys smelling of cut grass and sweat, I have their favorite cupcakes waiting. Their parents thank me without knowing a hint of my darker side. To all of them I don't need to be anything but a friendly, pudgy baker with a penchant for small talk, whose only need is the occasional compliment. I say let my old self remain where it belongs, back in that dingy apartment haunting the next round of tenants.

Briar agreed to come see the new house on Monday while Louis was still at work. I knew I had him, but did not know what to do with him.

Costume Dramas

$\mathcal{P}$eriod Piece Mondays were our weekly tradition. My sister was a connoisseur. She had seen everything from *Brideshead Revisisted* to *Upstairs, Downstairs*, and her collection kept growing. I was just a tourist, with little appreciation for history and having never read the classics, but that was how she liked it. This was a chance to get me cultured. The BBC version of *I, Claudius* — yeah, we watched all thirteen-thousand hours of it and the only good part was Livia and how she poisoned anyone who got in her way. As my sister put it, I've always had a thing for bitchy women in power. I told her that's why we get along so well.

Every Monday I'd drive down to Fairfax and she'd sequester her kids in the basement playroom. There was always wine, sometimes too much of it, and lots of takeout cartons. We'd eat and gossip until the conversation would naturally devolve into me ranting about my husband and whatever he had recently done to piss me off. To me, this was a form of bonding. She disagreed.

"The only drama I need right now is a costume drama," she'd say. That was her signal for me to stop talking and watch the film.

Needless to say, she was less than enthusiastic when I showed up one Monday evening holding a cheap bottle of merlot and a neatly packed suitcase. "Trouble at home?" she asked without a tinge of curiosity. I tried telling her that I wasn't permanently leaving my husband. I kept it simple: Ron's affair was a hypothetical. There was no act of infidelity. It was more of a feeling. He was sidetracked with life itself to the point that I wondered if his attention span had reached its capacity and was about to self-destruct. This was the best way of explaining what I'd hinted at for months.

My sister was a patient soul, part therapist, part fortune-teller, and one tough cookie. She was more interested in getting the nephews settled and the casserole out of the oven. "Save it for the costume drama," she said. That night's film was one of her favorites: the Gillian Anderson version of *House of Mirth*. That is what took priority.

On screen, we watched the downfall of Lily Bart. At first I was underwhelmed by the unpleasant drollness of it. Perhaps it was my limited understanding of scandal or my lack of sympathy for people who are oblivious to it. Lily Bart wasn't a likable character. She was weak and stupidly passive. But then, I'm the type of man who is also weak, passive and at times a little stupid. It wasn't until the end, when Selden ascended into her apartment, determined to marry her, to save her from herself, that I felt tenderness towards this sweet-natured woman who absentmindedly wandered into infamy. Selden was too late; Lily was already dead. As he muttered, "I love you," my sister echoed it under her breath.

"It's just like that," I said. "Ron is Selden and I'm Lily."

My sister gave me an exhausted look, as if I'd ruined the moment. She said the guestroom was ready but she needed to hide the sleeping draughts first.

After a month it was time to go home. I was tired of binging on period pieces, my nephews' antics and my sister's friends who treated her house like a large revolving door. Besides, my share of the mortgage was due and what was most disconcerting — Ron hadn't called. At first the silence had been disheartening, then offensive, but finally turned into full anxiety. Eventually he would call me. By the end of the month the anticipation of it followed me like a murderous shadow, knife unsheathed and the occasional stab to remind me it was still there.

At home, my husband greeted me at the door with an aloof smile. "There's been some changes since you've been gone," he said.

During my absence Ron had converted the garage into a rental unit. The previous owners had left it as a half-finished space with a small dilapidated bathroom and a nook for a kitchenette. For two years we had debated over its future: a master bedroom suite, a home office or theater. Now the harsh slab was carpeted and the kitchen was complete with glossy white appliances and vinyl countertops. Tucked in the corner lay a naked mattress next to a stack of boxes.

"Only took me a day to find a renter." Ron knew my need for privacy, my aversion towards strangers. The way I was guided around, it felt like I was expected to praise him for his handiwork. "I think you'll like Wayne," Ron said. "He's one of those artsy-types so you'll have plenty to talk about."

"How much are you charging?" He heard the resignation in my voice and I immediately regretted asking.

"Plenty. Now that you're back, I've got lots of options."

Jonathan Harper

$\mathcal{I}$ met the new tenant the following afternoon. Wayne was sickly-skinny with a greasy ponytail. Odors of sweat and turpentine clung to him. I hated him immediately: his nasally voice as gritty as his dirty fingernails, his habit of trailing off in thought mid-sentence. I could imagine a giant dust cloud following him everywhere. Around us the living room was cluttered with disorderly piles of tools and wood boards. My husband's trashy spy novels, the ones usually kept hidden in the attic, were stacked on the side. I asked Wayne what he was doing and he said, "Building a bookcase."

"Is Ron paying you for this?" I asked.

"Not really. We're deducting the cost from rent." When he crouched over, he wheezed out a little fart and glanced back, long enough to decide I wasn't the type who got offended by such things. That night I slept in the guestroom in order to escape the constant barrage of hammering.

Evidence of Wayne showed up everywhere, from his scattered tools to the ladies who scurried out the back door each morning. The guestroom shared a wall with the rental and I'd wake up to Wayne singing to himself while shuffling through his boxes. He farted constantly, with a machine-gun-type vibrato. In the afternoons Wayne worked on projects, all the little upgrades that Ron had talked about but never bothered starting: the bookshelf, the new crown molding, painting the garden shed. It was shoddy work at best, certainly not worth the deduction in rent. Some evenings I found Wayne and Ron together playing video games, slapping their controllers against their thighs over every defeat. Even when I didn't see Wayne the smell of turpentine lingered, a telltale sign he'd been over.

It was Wayne's art pieces that bothered me the most. He'd take up space in the driveway, using mounds of collected debris and welding them together into junky totems. He'd bring home wood crates, broken furniture, aluminum cans, anything he could use. One afternoon I discovered a lone toilet in the backyard. The bowl was cracked and full of what I hoped were rust stains. For weeks it sat there with weeds and grass growing around it until it looked like an artifact of some lost civilization. I hinted several times I wanted it gone. I called it gross and then a health hazard. Ron just laughed and told me the moment he caught Wayne using it he'd be sure to say something.

$\mathcal{F}$or Period Piece Mondays, we watched the *Bleak House* miniseries, in which Gillian Anderson played the regal and tragic Lady Dedlock.

Despite its bleakness, we managed to consume two bottles of Riesling as I described the ugly art pieces in all their nonsensical glory. My sister let me ramble on about the derelict toilet and the everlasting flatulence. But another glass of wine had me raving about how Ron and I were still not talking and how Wayne was ruining my life. That was when she told me to be quiet. We were missing an important part: Lady Dedlock, during her fabulous death scene, revealed that she was Esther's mother. When the episode finished, my sister uncorked a third bottle. She suggested I try befriending Wayne. Perhaps that would even the score.

*B*ut I wasn't sure which score needed to be settled. Ron was barely home. He'd stumble in late from his poker games and happy hours, each one of them a merry little distraction. The rent checks went straight to him to fund his weekend excursions. He'd disappear on Friday afternoon and return Sunday, sunburned or nursing a hangover. When he was home he was nothing but cordial. We still ate together on occasion, hovering over our plates with the evening game shows on. I asked him one night why we didn't see our friends anymore and he put on a mock-surprised face.

"What do you mean?" he asked. "I see them all the time!"

I still slept in the guestroom without complaint. Once or twice a week we had conjugal visits, these confusing acts that I initiated by crawling into our old shared bed, gently pulling back the covers with my teeth. When we finished, Ron would make an encouraging but sterile comment like, "That was nice," before curling up under the covers. I'd go back to the guestroom and fall asleep, serenaded by Wayne's farts and hammering.

*S*omehow, without realizing it, I began to adapt to this new norm of my household. I could still exist and take up space amidst the junk, the endless projects, the pleasant but distant smiles of my husband and his renter. If the endless Monday nights of period pieces had taught me anything, it was that history was full of people who waded through their lives in a state of discontentment and those who could not adjust to change were ultimately destroyed by it. I had become as resilient as Ron and knew it was only a matter of time before he recognized it.

But that all changed when Wayne bought his new car. I was home the afternoon a tow truck deposited it on the edge of our driveway. It was a beat-up 1979 Ford Ranchero with two flat tires. It looked downright dystopian,

Jonathan Harper

full of rust stains, dents, a dashboard full of steampunk levers and dials. The very sight of it repulsed me, like a rotting carcass, and released an oppressive anger that had me slamming doors and waiting until dark to come home. At least the dumpster-diving and renovation projects stopped; Wayne spent all his free time tinkering with his car. I was under the impression he knew very little about cars because he'd stand there with the hood up, gazing lovingly at the engine without ever doing anything to fix it. It was true romance for Wayne, far better than any lady friend he brought by to admire it.

One afternoon I found a long extension cord coming out of an opened window of the rental unit. It snaked across the front yard, down the driveway and connected under the Ranchero's hood. In the TV room, Wayne sat with Ron, watching the game while hunched over their beer and chicken wings.

"Wayne," I said, masking all evil intent, "what's going on with the power cord outside?"

Ron raised an eyebrow, but said nothing.

"Oh that," Wayne said after a prolonged silence. "Just charging the battery. That's all."

"What's our electricity bill going to look like?"

Wayne sat there scratching his balls and gave me a dopey-eyed look. This seemed incredibly difficult for him to put together. "Right… I'll look into that during the commercial."

$\mathscr{A}$t the start of Wayne's fourth month I crept into Ron's bedroom with the intention of having a serious chat. I wanted to tell Ron that I wasn't an idiot. I had obviously hurt him with my disappearing act and now he was punishing me. But I was reaching my limit and soon there wouldn't be anything left of us to salvage. I wanted him to know I was tired of the guestroom, tired of being ignored and that Wayne had to go.

But I didn't say any of that. Instead, I asked him to hit me. It was a moment of desperation. Ron look confused. "Spank me," I said. He gave me one weak slap. I crouched up on all fours. "Do it again, but hard." He struck; it barely stung. "Hurt me. With your belt."

"No. I'm not doing that." He rolled over on his side and I took the hint and left the room.

$\mathscr{I}$ didn't see Wayne the next day or the day after. The Ranchero still sat neglected at the end of the driveway. The latest junk totem, half built and poorly balanced, guarded the entrance to the rental unit's patio. It was an old floor lamp with a scaffold of wooden boards that held protruding light bulbs. Without thinking, I kicked it over and many of the bulbs shattered under its weight. Wayne didn't come home that night either.

After that I decided to change tactics. So I quit Period Piece Mondays, much to my sister's relief. That first Monday home, I ordered Chinese take-out, lured Ron into the TV room with lo mein and shrimp. He was kind enough not to mention the vandalism outside. It was just the two of us, the way I liked it, the game-show hosts our only companions.

"Where's Wayne?" I asked. When Ron shrugged I sighed. "It's so quiet here without him."

*G*lossy pink tickets started appearing on the Ranchero's wind-shield in rapid succession. The license plates hadn't been updated. I took the tickets inside and laid them flat on the desk in a row, wondering how many more until the county came to tow it away. I hadn't seen Wayne in two weeks and the totem hadn't been cleaned up either. At least Ron was staying home more often to fill the vacant space. On the surface he seemed to want things to change as well. To continue my Monday night tradition, he purchased a copy of *The Fall* miniseries, which was not a period piece but a modern crime drama set in Ireland. However, it starred Gillian Anderson as the De-tective Superintendent and that made me very happy. We sat and ate from little cardboard cartons while the heroine pursued a serial killer through the streets of Belfast. On these nights I felt a renewed contentment — not the old brilliant flames but a spark warm enough to comfort. I allowed myself to forget about the years of fighting and accusations. I truly believed that Wayne was the source of all our problems.

This lasted only a week.

By Friday night the house was once again deserted. Not even the mail had been brought in from the box. But I considered myself patient enough — I showered, ate and waited. Every room remained in an unnerving state of quiet to the point that I almost missed the noise of construction and flatu-lence. Finally I dialed Ron's number and, miraculously, he picked up.

"Where are you?" I asked.

"At the brewery," Ron called out. His voice mixed with the flood of back-ground music, streams of conversation and laughter. I couldn't remember

the last time I'd laughed with my husband. "All the guys say hello. They want to know where you've been," he said.

My stomach plummeted. "Tell them I'm here waiting."

He sighed deeply into the phone. "I'm sorry," he said. "I hardly thought you wanted to go out."

"Well, I did. It's Friday night and I came right home and waited for you."

I could hear him speak away from the receiver, could feel him push through the crowd as the background noise faded. Then he was outside, facing traffic. It was one of his pet peeves, having to leave the bar for a phone call. He always complained he was missing something inside.

"Can I tell you something?" he asked and without waiting for a response, he said, "I love you but you are the most miserable person I know. And when you're not trying to punish someone else, you punish yourself."

"Okay," I said.

"You have to learn that happiness is not something that is dished out with an ice cream scoop. And locking yourself up and avoiding everything doesn't make the world treat you any kinder."

"I'm sorry," I said.

"You have to decide whether you want to be happy or miserable. I will give you all the time you need to make your decision."

"But that's not fair," I cried out. I tried to reason with him, tried to explain that things had been bad between us for a long time and you can't will a problem out of existence.

"Maybe you should write that down in a letter. The guys are waving at me, so I need to go. You have a fun evening."

"But I'm all alone," I said.

"You'll figure something out." And then he hung up.

There was no sign of Wayne for another week. Each day a new ticket garnished his Ranchero. I searched the filing cabinet for his lease and his father was listed as an emergency contact. I sent a long wary email explaining the situation: his rent was due, his car would be towed, but at this point we were only interested in knowing if Wayne was all right. Without giving details, his father thanked me for my concern and assured me that his son would return eventually.

Another week passed.

Not knowing what else to do, I decided to write Gillian Anderson a fan letter. I figured, why not? This was a moment of desperation. Plus, I had seen enough of her work to know by now that she had a lot of experience with interpersonal relationships. I didn't want to be creepy so I decided to start by congratulating her on her recent films, including the cameo in *Tristram Shandy*, and how I thought it took a special sort of perseverance to find life after *The X-Files*. Then, I could gradually build enough trust so I could burden her with my problems. I wrote:

"Gillian, do you think Scully ever reached a breaking point with Mulder's conspiracy theories? Did she ever take this whole alien thing seriously? Would it have been wise for Scully to question his motives? Maybe it was all a cover-up for Mulder's own insecurities. Maybe he was just a bored man looking for a sense of purpose. Did it ever cross Scully's mind that he was going through a midlife crisis? And if so, would she have stayed with him?"

*I*t was after midnight, the night before Ron left for his yearly conference. I had been yanked out of pleasant dream. There had been a noise, like glass breaking or maybe the tumbling of boxes. It didn't matter. The house was quiet and I was too awake to simply fall back asleep. For a moment I was tempted to call my sister. We hadn't spoken in weeks. I wanted to know what new costume drama she'd recommend, to ask if she was still on speaking terms with her ex-husband. I wanted her to know there were still changes going on in my life and that they were important enough to warrant discussion. But it was late and Ron needed his sleep to catch his plane in the morning. Instead I put on the kettle and loaded the dishwasher. Our trash can was overflowing, so I took it outside to the bins.

Once outside, I noticed the little sconce light that hung over the rental unit's doorway. It was turned on. For the first time in weeks the patio was illuminated. I could see the telltale signs of Wayne littering the entrance: the cigarette butts, the dead potted plants and various pieces of scrap. A rusted screwdriver stuck out from the untamed grass. I wondered how long Wayne had been home, if he was still awake, and if this was my opportunity to collect his rent check before my husband could confiscate it.

Disregarding the late hour, I stepped over the debris and knocked on the door. It slid open. The rental unit was dark and I could barely detect the outline of furniture. When I called out no one answered. But I heard a small

Jonathan Harper

shuffling noise from somewhere within. I got the eerie feeling of some abandoned place. When I called out again, there was only silence.

"There's an intruder in the house," I said, shaking Ron out of the bed. He grunted in protest, curled further into the sheets. Then we heard the commotion, like a dozen boxes toppling over. That was enough for Ron to sit up and wipe the sleepiness from his eyes. We called the police.

Two officers arrived, both tall and pudgy and very sincere. They kept their guns secured in their holsters, flashlights in hand. They searched the unit for what felt like an unnecessarily long time while we remained out on the patio, Ron letting me lean against his chest. In the morning he'd be on a plane and I'd be left alone. "It's a total disaster in there," the officers told us. "Don't go in barefoot or you'll need a tetanus shot." Otherwise it was all clear and they suggested changing the locks.

We entered the rental unit and the destruction overwhelmed us. It was the first time in five months I'd stepped foot in it. The walls were chafed with long scratches and chunks of drywall were missing. It looked like a feral animal had been locked inside trying to gnaw its way out. Every available surface was covered by layers of dirty clothes, papers, dishes, cinder blocks, wood planks, gears, cut pieces of a chain-link fence. A capsized bottle of lube had drained out into a congealed dark spot on the carpet. The bathroom smelled of fermented piss. As we surveyed the wreckage minutes passed and I felt a paroxysm of claustrophobia. How could a man live like this? What if Wayne hadn't made it and he was buried underneath all the rubble? I wondered if the smell of him would linger on forever. And if so would his memory haunt us?

Of course Ron always had the better mind for drama. He was already locking the windows and picking up rusted nails from the floor. As I watched, it felt like I was seeing him for the first time, a disheveled but bold man, tired bags under his eyes, a slight drooping of his jowls. He gave me a quick apologetic look, as if he'd known all along this would happen. "Please don't leave me here alone," I said and tucked myself under his armpit, cheek pressed to the side of his chest. No matter what, he'd leave for the airport in the morning because his job, our livelihood, depended on it. But then, people ask their partners for the impossible all the time. I considered it a lover's challenge.

We Only Flinch
When It Isn't
Necessary

$\mathcal{G}$rant Bryce did not look good in a suit. While most people agreed that men his aged should clean up well, he was not the type and that was part of his charm. Years of living in Boulder had instilled in him an earthy ruggedness. His skin was tainted into a coarse olive complexion, his frame had widened with the slight definition of muscle. He never expected to find himself wandering aimlessly down the streets of his hometown dressed up like an overgrown school boy.

He wore a navy blue blazer over a creased Oxford shirt and a pair of pleated khaki trousers. This was the outfit his father, a man who valued appearances over authenticity, had purchased in anticipation of the summer's visit. Grant hated the sterile look of it, the formal red tie, the absurdity of the gold nautical buttons. It didn't help that the clothes didn't fit. The jacket's sleeves fell too short on his wrists while the pants hugged his waist and ankles. With each block, he felt his annoyance rise. What if he ran into someone he knew? This was not the impression he wanted to make. Back home he had spent a month hiking the Colorado Trail and a year working as the groundskeeper for an artist colony. No one would believe any of this if they saw him now. To him, the outfit was worse than ugly; it was a lie.

Grant had not seen his father in over a decade, which was enough time to accrue an ambivalent mixture of resentment and longing for him. He had grown up in a small suburb outside Washington, D.C., and was quite certain that at one time he had been happy here. There was a faint memory of walking hand-in-hand with his parents along the reflecting pool towards the Lincoln Memorial. The image juxtaposed with another: he was eight years old, eyes puffy from crying, but happily eating a gyro in a restaurant booth while his father smiled at him apologetically. He could not remember the circumstances that had made him cry. There was a slideshow of other memories as well: the morning his father had taken him to be baptized in secret, his mother reading tarot cards at the dining room table, the mysterious kitchen fire that remained a family controversy for years, even though both parents refused to discuss it with him.

For months this reunion between father and son had loomed ahead, growing fat with expectation. Grant wanted to feel overwhelmed with sentimentality and nostalgia. He also wanted the summer visit to hurt one of them. Perhaps both. This happened, but not in the way he had anticipated. His father's presence was as suffocating as the suit and when the moment came to escape Grant took it. Now he found himself wandering aimlessly down Broad Street with the battered pride of a teenage runaway.

"It wasn't supposed to be like this," he said to a woman walking a cocker spaniel. She nodded in agreement, the way one did to a retarded person, enough to show sympathy but not encourage further conversation.

Around him the cafés were starting to fill. Sunday services were over and the church crowds were now infesting the streets. Somewhere his father was among them.

Grant turned off the main road and into the northern neighborhoods. At first he couldn't have said where he was going. He moved by instinct, retracing his old steps from childhood until he reached a familiar cul-de-sac, sweaty and breathless, staring wistfully ahead at the small brick house in the back. His lungs filled with delirious nostalgia. When he rang the bell there was a sudden frenzy of activity inside. The drapes ruffled and the door creaked open, its chain lock still fastened.

Grant paused, suddenly unsure of why he had come here. "It's me," he said. The door closed, the lock was undone and then it reopened.

In the doorway stood Mr. Lunch Copeland, mouth buckled and eyes as wide as eggs. Years ago Lunch had been Grant's Sunday School teacher and confidant. Back then he had near mythic qualities: a sort of suburban Viking, the kind of childhood guardian only found in children's books. Now he was looked old and bloated, his once wavy red hair thinning out. His neck drooped into sagging folds that would need scaffolding to fix.

"You remember me, right?" Grant asked.

Those egg eyes widened. "Yup. Been a long time."

"Aren't you going to invite me in?"

Lunch scratched himself through his baggy shorts and glanced at the other houses. No one was around, so he ushered Grant inside.

The den was full of birdcages: Victorian oval-headed cages, box-cut bamboo cages, little pedestal cages. All of them ornate, the collection covering every available surface, a few standing, others suspended like common houseplants, until the room itself became a vacant aviary. There had never

Jonathan Harper

been any birds. There was, however, a boy. He sat shirtless on the tweed couch staring vacantly into the television.

"Say hello, Sam. This here is an old friend of mine," Lunch said and intertwined his fingers into a cat's cradle.

The boy didn't even look up. "Can we watch *Blade Runner* again? That's a good film."

"Go ahead and start it. I'm going to get us some drinks."

Grant was not happy being left behind. The den took on a disturbing quality. It was nothing like what he remembered. Most of the cages were in need of repair. Some of the bars looked twisted out. The room was incredibly dusty. He felt the last drops of nostalgia evaporate within him as he watched Sam rummage through the scattered DVDs. The boy looked both innocent and terrible, an ugly child losing badly in the early rounds of his fight with puberty. There was a fierce territorial quality in the way Sam tossed the movie cases aside. He gave off the impression of an overgrown rodent gnashing its teeth.

"Can I help you?" Sam asked.

Grant realized he was staring. "No. You can't," he said.

In the kitchen, Lunch sat at the dinette, face scrunched up in a way that made his neck puff out. He had two water glasses waiting. An oppressive amount of light poured in from the small window. The room felt too bright.

"I guess I should have expected this," Lunch said. "None of you ever came back before, but it was bound to happen."

Grant took his glass but did not drink. "How old is he? Twelve? Thirteen?"

Lunch cleared his throat, a guttural phlegm-filled noise like a clogged drain. It warned: *Be quiet. Voices travel far in small houses.*

"He's eighteen. And that's the only answer I'll give."

"Bullshit." Grant took his seat. When he was Sam's age, he had sat in this same spot, eating pudding cups while listening to Jim Morrison sing off a vinyl record. The kitchen used to have a calming effect, something that hovered over you long after you left.

"I never hurt you," Lunch said.

Grant flushed. "What do you mean?"

"I need you to acknowledge it. I never hurt you."

In the next room, the television rose a notch.

"I never would have hurt you," Lunch repeated.

"I know that," Grant said. The nostalgia was replaced with a slow build of panic. He had come to see Lunch because he needed help. Because two hours ago he had leapt out of his father's car and had nowhere else to go.

"You need to understand. You were my little boy. I never would have hurt you. I protected you. I kept you safe." Lunch stared forward. His egg eyes looked ready to crack.

And Grant whispered, "Then please, do it again."

This was not the first time Grant had asked for sanctuary. He was fourteen when his parents divorced. The combination of his father's newfound religion and his mother's rebellion against all things pious had created such a destructive force in his life that he accepted the news with a sigh of relief. But when his mother announced she was taking him with her to Colorado, Grant absconded to Lunch's house. With the naïvety of the young he had expected an invitation to stay, to become a permanent fixture in the little cottage and never have to see his parents again. Instead his host calmly shook his head. "You're getting too old for this," Lunch told him. "You should go to Colorado while you have the chance." That was a very evangelical day.

Grant's current problems were far more convoluted. He knew that it had all started when he was accepted into a graduate program at Penn State. After years of dwindling communication, his father had contacted him. The invitation to come visit was clear and unambiguous: Grant should stay with him until he was ready to go to Pennsylvania. His father explained it would be easier to find housing if he were already on the East Coast. This had sparked a fantasy in Grant's mind. While the circumstances remained unclear, he pictured himself sitting across from his father in a posh hotel bar, sipping top-shelf liquor. In this scene, his father handed him an Ed McMahon-sized check to cover his tuition as well as the keys of his prized Mustang while Grant took the pleasure of refusing all of it.

Instead, when he arrived home there was a severe formality to his reunion. His father's handshake was austere as he introduced his wife and two daughters, all of them acting like they were governed by some omnipresent force and were afraid to draw too much attention to themselves. There was no talk of the previous decade, of Penn State or financial support. Instead, he had been whisked away to the formal dining room where his father dictated two topics of conversation.

The first was that he had arranged an interview for Grant at his law firm. "It's just a formality," Mr. Bryce said. "We've put together an administrative position. You can start next week." When Grant reminded him he was leaving soon, his father dismissed it with a wave of his hand. The summer was just beginning and he should be thankful for the job. How else could he afford an apartment without the first month's rent?

The second topic was more disturbing, because it was introduced at random. The historic Great Falls Church had recently defected from the Episcopal Diocese and Mr. Bryce bragged that he was the lawyer who made it all possible. The new congregation was now in total control of the property and monetary assets while the continuing Episcopals were barred from the premises. The local newspaper had turned it into an overblown scandal, but that wasn't something Grant should worry about. As if to prevent any questions, his father began lecturing on property laws and the rights of a local congregation.

The next morning Grant felt fully absorbed into the family's bosom. Mr. Bryce woke him early in time for services and presented him with the ugly church clothes. Soon Grant found himself crammed in the backseat of a station wagon, a sister's elbow jabbing his side for more room. He had no recollection of how he got there. In fact, it felt like he had not been in control of his own actions all morning. While his father had not commanded or forced him, there been a series of gentle pushes in the right direction, as if Mr. Bryce knew that any delay would allow Grant to regain control over his senses. A blast of nausea hit him in the gut.

"Pull over," Grant had said. The car sped up to beat a red light. In the distance, he could see the church. He felt like he was being hurtled towards it. "Let me out," he said. He felt claustrophobic and then enraged that his father ignored him. One of the girls leered at him while his stepmother robotically stared out the window. At the final intersection Grant opened the car door while his father turned back, yelling incomprehensibly. The truck in the next lane stopped short and honked and Grant took off running down the street, leaving them all far behind him.

"I'm surprised people are still talking about that," Lunch said later on. "So much fuss over one fag bishop." It was the only thing Lunch ever said about the defection.

They were seated in the darkened aviary. *Blade Runner* played on the television. Lunch sat aloof in his arm chair, almost seething in his discomfort, eyes darting between the movie and his two young guests. On occasion Grant would meet his gaze and Lunch would look away. Sam was the only one who seemed at peace. He lounged in the center of the couch, brittle legs sprouting out at awkward angles. On screen Decker pursued the red-haired replicant through a labyrinth of alleyways.

"This part's important," Sam said. "This is where you can tell that Decker has no humanity." Then Decker shot the replicant as she ran screaming through panes of glass.

Grant rolled his eyes. "Right," he muttered. The boy had talked through half the film.

"He murders her. This makes the movie." Sam was staring at him.

"She's an android. She's killed people and she knows she's illegal on Earth," Grant said flatly. He wished the boy would go away.

"But so is Decker. He's a replicant, too. He just doesn't know it yet. He murders one of his own!"

"No, he isn't. I've seen this movie a dozen times."

"He is too — it's because of the unicorn fantasies," Sam protested. "I read that online." The boy looked very severe, as if he just taught everyone a valuable lesson.

When the film ended Sam put his shirt back on, waved with a newfound camaraderie, and left through the mudroom. His head bounced by the kitchen window and gave one last farewell smile before he disappeared.

Lunch stumbled back into the kitchen. "You must be hungry." He disassembled a package of deli meat and spread wads of mayonnaise onto slices of white bread. "I hope you're not still a vegetarian."

Grant shook his head politely. He felt a sudden impulse to rush up and embrace Lunch. He wanted to be cradled in the man's lap, head tucked under Lunch's chin. The moment passed.

"Good. I figured that was just a stage." Lunch set out plates and uncapped two bottles of Corona. "How is your mother doing?" he asked.

"Fine. Still lives in Boulder and weirder than ever. She's taken up a lot of New Age stuff. Yoga and shit, but it makes her happy." He ate frantically.

"And your father?"

"Still the same horrible man," Grant mumbled while chewing.

"Yeah, I see him around. How long are you here for?"

The beer had already gone warm in his hand; he wanted to feel a buzz but didn't. "That would be a source of contention," he said. "I thought it was for a few days. Apparently, Dad didn't."

Lunch nodded. "Ah, the root of the problem, I see. This is what you were arguing about?"

"No. It's more complicated than that." As he explained the morning's events leading up to his escape, his motives felt childish. It couldn't have been as simple as him just not wanting to attend mass. "I wasn't given a choice," Grant said. "I was in the car, dressed up in someone else's clothes, and it felt like they were hurrying me along so I couldn't stop to think about what was happening. I'm supposed to go to grad school and no one's even mentioned that. I honestly thought I was being indoctrinated."

Then he got quiet. It was easy to forget that Lunch was still affiliated with the congregation, even if he wasn't puritanical about it. Grant downed the rest of his Corona and found Lunch inspecting him oddly, barely concealing his smile with his cupped hands.

"What is it?" Grant asked.

"I'm admiring the man you've become." Lunch arched back in his chair and lazily brought his bottle to his lips. "You're a man now, all grown up."

Grant blushed — he didn't want to feel grown up. He imagined a large gruff hand, more like a bear claw, cuffing the back of his neck and scruffing the skin like one does a kitten.

"It amazes me what I see kids turn into. The cruel ones, they stay the same for many years and they never really think beyond the moment. It's the nice ones who change. They always grow into their personalities."

"Was I one of the good ones or the bad ones?"

"You were the sweetest one of them all. So gentle. Very conscientious and considerate of other people's feelings. You were also the most timid little person I'd ever met. It looked like you tested the ground wherever you walked to make sure it wouldn't crumble under your feet. And look at you now. Taking a stand."

Grant smiled into his empty bottle, not wanting to second-guess anything. But then his face tightened and he was unable to look up. "How many others were there?" he asked and heard Lunch suck in air through the gap in his front teeth.

"Only a few. It takes a certain level of trust to really build a friendship."

We Only Flinch When It Isn't Necessary

"How long has Sam been coming here?"

"Not long." Lunch shifted in his chair with a low grunt. "He reminds me a lot of you when you were his age. Not nearly as polite, but he's very perceptive. He isn't doing well in school and I know he gets bullied." As Grant began to speak, Lunch hushed him. "Sam and I haven't spent a lot of quality time together. Like I said, it takes a lot of trust to build a friendship. And I want to help him, protect him, but right now I'm not under the impression he's capable of that level of trust."

"How did you find him?"

"Same I way I found you. He was one of my students, though his family doesn't attend anymore."

They were silent for several minutes.

"Do you have anyone special in your life?" Lunch asked and Grant shook his head. "That's a shame. Guys your age should have lots of sweethearts."

"I dated a few girls back home. In fact, they called me a serial monogamist. I was even with a man for a while." He noted Lunch's discomfort. "It was a very brief relationship, but an intense one. He reminded me of you, a little. But it wasn't what I was looking for."

Lunch began collecting the empty bottles and plates. He did not offer anything else. "You should go back to college. Get your PhD," he said. "If you came here looking for permission, you don't need it. You have the potential."

"May I stay here tonight? Just tonight. On the couch?"

Lunch shook his head. "No, I don't think that's a good idea. But you should visit again before you leave. Maybe next Sunday. He doesn't show it well, but Sam really liked you." The old man, acting through old habits, opened the back door to the mudroom. "Like old times," he said. It meant that Grant needed to leave. Discreetly. Neighbors tended to pry.

"There are things we need to discuss," Mr. Bryce said, following Grant into the basement guestroom. His stepmother was two steps behind, trying to intervene with her talent for peacemaking, but she was blocked by the closing door.

As Grant tossed the ugly blazer into the armoire, he cringed at the sour smell of his underarms. His shirt felt drenched in sweat. "Can you give me a moment to change?" Grant asked.

Jonathan Harper

His father was a ridiculous man. He had the tenacity of an enraged but feeble ostrich, the type of man to flinch immediately after throwing a punch. He moved in between Grant and the guestroom's bath and said, "I will not be ignored."

"I'm warning you," Grant said and watched his father's eyes widen. "I'm pretty gross right now." He had pulled off the trousers and was unbuttoning his shirt. Mr. Bryce looked flustered and turned his head away to avoid seeing his son in his underwear.

"I am enforcing a few rules for the remainder of your stay. For starters, no more jumping out of cars like an idiot daredevil! You could have caused an accident." As he said this he tossed his hands about in an agitated fashion and started to pace. "For that matter, you will not disappear whenever you like. We have a strict order here. All members of the family will be present for dinner each night and church on Sunday morning. That is not negotiable."

Grant sat on the edge of his bed in nothing but his boxer shorts. He crossed his arms and contemplated the absurd outline of his short, dumpy father, pacing back and forth. His old man was practically ranting, going on about how he loved his son and felt the distance between the two had allowed for unfair judgments on both sides. Though he could not be specific, he was under the the impression that Grant had been influenced by unscrupulous forces throughout his life and as a result made very poor decisions.

"There were no conditions when you first invited me here," Grant reminded him. Then, without thinking, he dipped his hand into his shorts and pulled his sweating balls from his thighs. His father balked.

"Stop doing that," Mr. Bryce snapped. He looked queasy.

"I had an itch."

"The itch is long gone. Now you're just having a party down there."

Grant let out a little chirp. He was almost enjoying himself now.

"I know you prefer your mother to me," Mr. Bryce said, "but she's full of nonsense. And she raised you with my money and not my values. Now that you're here, you will finally follow my rules." His voice exhausted itself into a pitiful air cloud.

"All right, Dad. Then I'll make sure this is a very short visit," Grant replied.

And that was enough. His father bowed his head, almost grieving the moment. "You're going to be all alone one day if you're not careful," he said and then paused as if to reflect on his wisdom. "When you're ready, my wife left

We Only Flinch When It Isn't Necessary

some dinner for you upstairs." Leaving, Mr. Bryce turned and slammed the door behind him.

The guestroom opened into the basement playroom. It was full of discarded furniture and childhood relics: the pink Fisher Price oven set that collected dust, shelves full of old Disney films and forgotten board games. When he finally emerged, all cleaned up, he found his sisters huddled together on the loveseat, whispering. Delores, the stepsister, fidgeted with the TV remote in an attempt to control her nervous fingers. She was fourteen, a plump girl with a soft blushing face. Wendy, the half-sister, openly sneered at him, her boney legs resting on the family's golden retriever as if it were a piece of furniture. She was only ten but somehow possessed the judgmental glare of an old woman.

Upon seeing the two girls together, he hesitated in the doorway. This was their territory, the playroom — even though both of them seemed too old for such a thing. Still, he was surprised by the sudden realization that he felt intimidated. Not necessarily by his sisters but by kids in general. For as long as he could remember he had no tolerance for anything that represented childhood. He disapproved of their uncensored behaviors, their lack of awareness and consequence. Worse, he cringed at the thought of himself at that age, convinced he had been the most embarrassing child of them all. It was a brief moment, but he pushed past it, walked forward and said good evening.

"Did you hear something? It sounded like a fart," Wendy said, flapping her wrist.

Delores sighed. "Did you want to watch TV with us?" Her almond-shaped mouth curved into an apologetic smile.

Grant shook his head, but before he could continue upstairs the golden retriever crawled out from beneath Wendy's feet, panting happily towards him.

"Midas! Come back here," Wendy snapped as the dog nuzzled Grant's palm. "Stupid mutt, come back here this instant," she hissed. She lunged forward and pulled the poor beast by its collar back to the couch. Delores's head remained bowed, watching her fingers methodically rub little circles around the remote buttons, not looking up once.

Grant went upstairs and ate off a cold plate before returning to his room. The girls ignored him this time, but even with the door shut he could hear the television and Wendy's high-pitched cackle. So much for privacy, he

Jonathan Harper

thought and fell onto the bed. The comforter beneath him laid out a grid of brown squares with little patterns of red poppies. The wood bedposts stood sentinel, filled with distressed fissures. He fell asleep thinking about Lunch.

$\mathcal{T}$he next morning he lay in bed listening to the family upstairs trying to organize itself for the day. Toilets flushed and showers ran in rapid succession, followed by the chaotic fumbling in the kitchen. He heard Wendy stomping downstairs to the basement, singing to herself. When he emerged, his wispy hair sticking out like a dark halo. Wendy told him he stank. Playfully, he angled his armpit over her and she slapped at him. "You're a pervert," she yelled. Thankfully, both parents had already left for work.

Grant set up his computer, an outdated desktop, and browsed through rental ads up in Pennsylvania. Students were still vacating the college town in a mass exodus. Within the hour he had emailed a dozen inquiries, each one a new hope that the remainder of the summer could be salvaged. Then he disassembled the computer and fit the pieces back into their packing foam just as Wendy crept back downstairs, visibly irritated that she couldn't take a turn on the Internet.

Feeling accomplished, Grant took the dog for a walk and the nostalgia returned. His old neighborhood was exactly the same and yet it wasn't. Children were everywhere, the summer break turning them feral. The dog led him through his familiar route along the old bike path and up towards the shops on Broad Street, where the elderly window-shoppers paused and let Midas lick their hands. He didn't plan to stop at Lunch's house, just walk by it enough times as to remind his old friend he had not disappeared again, should Lunch be sitting at his window. But when he tried to head north into the next subdivision, Midas tugged him further away, where the old video rental and arcade had once been. Now it was a brick office building with a bank at street level.

The used bookstore was still in the same wooden shack with its faded murals painted over the entrance. Seeing it brought back a terrible memory: the day the owner had caught him shoplifting old *Playboys*. His friends wore large jackets (quite suspicious for summer) and would slip the magazines under their shirts while Grant asked to see the little red hardbacks kept in the display case. Of course the old woman had a third eye for mischief and before the first magazine was secreted away all of them were in her clutches, standing in a dejected row while she called their parents. Except Grant's were with the marriage counselor and she had to leave a message. He ran crying all the way to Lunch's house. He remembered being cradled against the man's bare chest, hearing Lunch's soft chuckle over his own sobs. "There's nothing wrong with a little curiosity," Lunch had told him. "But you know if you get caught, you got to pay the price." What Grant remembered most about this moment was the tingling sensation of callused fingers rubbing through his hair and grazing his scalp. Nothing ever felt as soothing.

Further down, he paused briefly before the neon "Open" sign of a coffee shop. It took him a moment to realize that this had once been Kristy's Coffee Parlor, full of wicker chairs and amateur art with bright custard-colored walls. He remembered it as a loud jovial place where he had squandered his allowance on milkshakes, while Kristy herself floated ethereally amongst her guests. Now it was a formal grid of square tables, where laptop users all typed quietly in perfect synchronicity. He left Midas tied out front to the guard rail and hunkered down next to the front bay windows with a mug of iced coffee. It felt very adult to sit there.

He locked eyes with a middle-aged woman holding a clipboard. She stood idling in the back of the parlor, but once she gazed upon him she walked forward. "Excuse me, sir. Do you have a moment?" she asked and forced a piece of paper into his hand. She didn't wait for a response. "As you may know, recently the Great Falls Church was taken over by evangelical separatists and this has greatly shaken the community." Her tone was mechanical, as if she were reciting a programmed script, pointing a well-manicured fingernail into the flier. It was crudely printed on offensively bright orange paper, the words FIGHT BACK AGAINST THE COUP on top in bold letters. At first Grant thought she was deranged, but then he realized she was referencing his father's church. It was indeed a scandal, but she described it as some draconian conspiracy: secret meetings had taken place and now the historic church grounds themselves were being held hostage.

"Look, this doesn't have anything to do with me. I'm just visiting," he said.

The woman fidgeted. Her concentration seemed momentarily shattered. "But this has ramifications for all of us. Surely you know someone who is affected."

"My father," he started to say and then got quiet. She asked him who his father was but Grant quietly shook his head.

The woman sat down, but was careful not to brush against him. Strangely, this made her seem less intrusive. "Listen to me carefully," she said. "I'm not

a religious fanatic. I'm not some born-again ex-junkie or a conspiracy theorist. I'm not a literal believer. But I was betrayed — this was a community I wanted to raise my daughter in. And a group of people came in and took it away from us." Her tone was calm and mournful. As she spoke, he felt she could be describing anything: a community garden or a shared piece of jewelry. He looked over the flier. A list of names appeared, the ones most responsible for the defection, and two stood out. The first was his father, Mr. Terrence Bryce, and the second Mr. Lunch Copeland.

"What was the reason they gave for defecting?" he asked.

"Biblical inerrancy." She said it like it was a disease.

He signed his name, gloating quietly as he wrote his father's address on the mailing list.

*H*e arrived home later than he should. Midas barked as the family congregated in the dining room. Wendy, who was folding paper napkins, dramatically wrapped her arms around the dog's neck. "Where did he take you? Are you okay?" She glared vengefully at Grant. "Don't you ever run off with my dog again!"

He sat and folded his unwashed hands for the grace-before-meals. The prayer was quick and pointless but pleasant enough. When he was younger, in those last few months before the divorce, his father had tried introducing this ritual. Grant and his mother had exchanged dry looks, both holding in their giggles at the new family experiment. As his father said, "Amen," the family repeated it in unison. Across the table, Wendy scowled. She slipped pieces of chicken under her seat to the begging dog. She said, "Midas has been traumatized! Look, he's still hiding under my chair!"

"Yes, dear. Very traumatized," Mrs. Bryce said.

After a suitable amount of time, Grant spoke up. "Today was a productive day."

His father cleared his throat and speared a Brussels sprout with his fork. "Really?"

"I sent out a ton of emails for apartments. I'll check again tomorrow, but chances are I'll be driving up this week to sign a lease."

"Good," Wendy muttered, but everyone ignored her.

"What about the job interview?" Mr. Bryce said. His wife placed a soft hand upon his shoulder, quietly shaking her head.

Grant paused to examine the mess of his dinner plate and pushed his food into orderly mouthfuls. "I'm afraid I don't have time. Apartments go fast and I want to get settled as quickly as possible." He returned a pleasant smile to his stepmother and watched her hand recede from Mr. Bryce's shoulder.

"I'd like to go, too," Delores said shyly. "If it's all right, I'd like to see the mountains."

The table went silent except for the awkward sound of chewing.

"It's a pretty long drive and you'd be bored," Grant finally said. "There won't be anything for you to do. It'll be all apartment hunting and job interviews." Delores frowned and continued to pick at the chunks of dried-out chicken.

"Well, it sounds like you had a productive day after all," his father grumbled and cleared his plate.

On Thursday Grant drove up to Pennsylvania and inspected three rental opportunities but ended up signing a lease on a fourth that had serendipitously become available. The scheduled move-in date was the following week. He took the long way home through the curvy mountain passes that intersected little towns while his car stuttered along. He stopped at a farmer's market in a wooden pavilion with chipped white paint and was struck by the neatly organized rows of fruit. He imagined making weekly shopping trips out there and purchased a small bag of nectarines, eating them as he drove.

At the dinner table his stepmother flattered him with conversation. (Mr. Bryce took his meal into the study.) She was pleased about the recent developments. "It sounds like you got a great deal," she said while passing the serving bowl. Grant vividly described the apartment and lied about several job prospects, while the two girls ate in silence. "You're going to do great in school," his stepmother continued. "I can tell all my friends we'll have a doctor in the family."

He stayed hidden in the guestroom for the remainder of his stay. It was comfortable enough, though there was a persistent nagging in the back of his mind and he would check his cell phone, half-expecting Lunch to have called even though they hadn't exchanged numbers. Otherwise he lay out on the bed, listening to the happenings upstairs. He assembled and disassembled his computer. He compulsively masturbated. He took Midas on a short walk and still Wendy berated him afterwards. Once and only once,

Delores had shyly tapped the guestroom door, calling for him. When she pushed it open, he feigned sleep while she watched him. When he finally turned over, she was gone, leaving the door ajar. His father avoided him throughout the weekend.

It was Sunday morning and he was exhausted from stewing in his raw emotions for so long. Why hadn't his father come down? It was like the old man had flipped a switch and tuned out all apathy, anything that derailed from his vision of the good, right and true. Grant was sitting upright in bed, staring angrily at the closed door. The guestroom had become a sort of time capsule where he felt his younger self wallowing after a temper tantrum. There was an illusion of half-built LEGO structures, ruffled picture books, and a worn-out teddy bear to which he had confided his secrets. Now he couldn't shake the naked association between his father and some oppressive backwoods zealot and yet he wanted the opportunity to decline any offer of reconciliation. The ghostly visage of his younger self nodded its approval.

When the door did open, he grabbed his book and pretended to read. But he was caught off guard to see both sisters in the doorframe, posed in their church clothes. Delores's dress wrapped around her defensively, her body drenched in a lilac floral print that accentuated her chubbiness. Wendy looked like a sun child, a yellow skirt with a bright orange top, propping her little chest fiercely towards him.

"Mom said you'd be hiding in here. We're leaving in ten minutes." Wendy glanced at him as if she was disgusted. "You smell awful," she added.

Delores seated herself at the writing desk, hands smoothing out her dress. "You'll miss brunch afterwards. You can still come to that, right?" she asked. Since arriving, he'd resisted his impulse to like her.

"No praise, no glaze," Grant said and looked back down at the book.

Wendy placed a hand on her shapeless hip and then plucked the novel out of his hand before tossing it across the room. "We all have to go," she said. "What makes you so special?"

"Why are you here?" Grant asked. He kept looking past them in hopes that his father was eavesdropping outside the door.

"Mom calls you a lost soul. You should really be with us today," Delores added.

That last remark stung. "Your mother doesn't know what she's talking about." He could feel the anger inside begin to bubble. "She's like a parrot. She repeats whatever she's told."

"You don't even know our mother," Wendy snapped.

Delores clutched the edge of her dress and twisted it in her curled hands. "Mom says that you're family. And that's important."

"No, he isn't." Wendy hadn't moved out of his face. She was peering at him with the same sadistic enthusiasm as a small boy burning ants under a magnifying glass. He told them he would be leaving the next morning and then none of it would matter. "Good," Wendy said.

The anger continued to rise as he glared back at her. "There's a lot going on here I don't want to be a part of and you're either too young or stupid to understand any of it." Wendy called him a brat and he could feel himself losing grip on his calm demeanor. Every bit of aggression he had reserved for his father now redirected towards her. "I want nothing to do with you or your mother. She was having an affair with my dad and the reason my parents got divorced was because she got pregnant with you." Both girls stared, Wendy too confused to quit smiling. "Did you hear me? You're a bastard child and your mom's a whore. So I don't care what she thinks of me."

But was it true? Grant had always known this, even though it had never been officially confirmed. It was the kind of belief that seemed logical enough to be a truth.

Wendy's smile evaporated, her forehead furrowed and mouth clenched with scornful indentations. "You're a dick," she said. "Do you hear me? You're a dick!" She yelled the last part and ran out of the room.

He wondered if he should chase after her, if there was certain protocol when you spoke this way to a child. It was possible she didn't even know what a bastard was outside of being one of the lesser curse words. But he knew she had been jostled out of the safety net of childlike resilience. He might as well have grabbed her around the neck and squeezed. Then he glanced over at Delores with the dim realization that she was still seated at the desk. She seemed to shrink and become concave, her mortified fingers scrunching up her dress as if ready to tear through the fabric. "That's not true," she whimpered. "Why would you say such a horrible thing?" Her plump face dipped as waves of brown curls fell over her eyes, making her look even more delicate.

"Of course it's not true," he lied. He noticed her tears. He wanted to comfort her, but not hold her. "I'm sorry — I'm saying stupid shit because I'm unhappy," he told her. "Please don't start crying."

Jonathan Harper

Delores shook her head from beneath her bangs and then he recognized in her the only ally he had in this household. He imagined them in the future, meeting for a drink, Delores a full-figured woman wearing a black dress. He saw her as a husky beauty, a roaring twenties jazz singer with a feathered clip in her hair. She would be the type of independent woman who worked with orphans and old people and the next moment gossip frantically while waving a cigarette. He wished, suddenly, that he had taken her with him up to Pennsylvania for the day.

His stepmother came in to investigate the shouting. "Is everything all right?" she half-sang. Delores didn't say anything. Instead, she threw herself towards the door and locked her arms around her mother's waist. Grant stared over at his book, lying limp against the far wall, its pages crumpled. He knew it was time to go.

$\mathcal{B}$y the time Mr. Bryce returned from services, the only sign his son had been there was the lone suit hanging in the guestroom armoire. Grant had quickly thrown his boxes into his car's trunk, wondering what tale his father would spin about the covert departure. But he was not ready to leave town yet. Even though he knew he would be refused, he wanted to spend his last night at Lunch's house. He wanted to rekindle with something. "One last favor and I'll be gone forever, I promise," he kept repeating to himself as he drove.

The backdoor was always unlocked for special visitors and Grant crept in through the mudroom. At first the house appeared empty. But as he entered the den he found Sam sprawled out on the couch, all alone and unattended.

"Where's Lunch?" Grant asked and the boy jumped up in his seat with a startled wide-eyed look. The left side of his face was heavily bruised, his eyeball swollen with broken capillaries and glossy from a layer of mucus. A gash in his bottom lip was sealed by three stitches.

After a long pause, Sam rolled over and buried his face into the couch. "Aren't you going to ask what happened to me?"

"I'm sorry. You caught me off guard," Grant said. "Are you all right?"

"No. I got jumped on the walk home the other day," Sam grumbled. "I got band camp tomorrow and everyone'll see me like this."

Seeing the distressed boy, his injuries, the darkened aviary — it all filled him with a sense of trespass. The boy eyed him from the edge of a throw pillow. It was a perverse little plea for sympathy. If he had not exploded on his sisters, he might have turned around and left. But instead, he felt a sense of obligation. Grant squatted down and gently touched Sam's jaw, rubbing a thumb over the bruise. The boy did not resist. His bulbous eye stared forward.

"It's already fading — it'll look even better by tomorrow." Grant looked around, half-expecting Lunch to emerge from some hiding place. He wondered if this was a test and if so, had he passed it. "Does it hurt? Do you want some ice?"

"Ice won't do shit."

"Okay, then let's sit in a dark room and do nothing," Grant snapped. The boy scrunched himself back into a fetal position and began to pout. "Please don't get upset," he said. He patted the boy on the back, knowing these little dramatic acts would soon get exhausting. "Do you know where Lunch is? When's he coming back?"

"Church. It's Sunday." The boy's eyes darted side-to-side conspiratorially. "Why are you here?"

"I just wanted to say goodbye." He let there be a little pause. "It looks like we're both in the same boat. Do you want to watch a movie while we wait for him?"

He put on *Blade Runner* again and left Sam wrapped in a throw blanket as he paced through the kitchen. He couldn't shake the feeling that they were being watched, as if through a crystal ball. A bottle of gin collected dust on top of the fridge, tempting him. He took a few sips and wandered to the den where the movie glowed eerily from the screen, illuminating the little boy and the dangling cages. Grant imagined Sam as an exotic bird in a cage who was in danger of someone plucking out all his delicate feathers.

"Aren't you going to sit with me?" the boy asked. Grant did, reluctantly. "How often did you come here?"

"That was a long time ago," Grant said. "Before my parents got divorced, my mom gave me money and sent me out for the day because of all the fighting. I used to go to this coffee shop on Broad Street and when the money ran out, I came here."

Sam smiled sheepishly while Decker battled androids in the background. "We talked about you all week. He told me you moved to the mountains and you had horse farms and rattlesnakes and huge blizzards every winter. He made you sound prolific. Like a cowboy."

Jonathan Harper

"I think you mean 'exotic' and I'm not a cowboy. I always thought I was Oliver Twist," Grant said. They sat quietly for a bit. Neither seemed interested in the movie. "Why aren't you in church?"

"We got kicked out. So we don't go anymore."

The movie ended and Lunch still hadn't returned. When Sam went to the bathroom, he used the one upstairs. The boy knew the upstairs — how much trust had that required, Grant wondered. He made them peanut butter sandwiches and poured iced tea from the pitcher. He pissed and squeezed out a little turd in the washroom off the kitchen. It was mid-afternoon. There was no reason for Lunch to be gone so long. By now the church crowds had vacated the shops on Broad Street. Everything felt wrong.

"Come on. We're leaving," Grant said. Sam creased his brow and shook his head, but Grant had already pulled him to his feet and ushered him towards the back door. "Put on your shirt. We shouldn't be here all by ourselves." It surprised him that Sam obeyed.

They drove down to the coffee shop. The afternoon rush had trickled out and now there were only a few typists behind laptops. They drank aggressively and left their tea bags on little marked-up piles of paper. As Grant approached the counter, the barista smiled brightly before she stammered, "What happened to your face?" Sam angrily turned away.

"I think he wants a smoothie," Grant told her.

They took a small table in the back near the restrooms, where Sam shifted uncomfortably in his chair, glancing over his shoulder every few moments. A group of skateboarders passed the front bay window and he shrank low. When Grant asked if he knew them, Sam said he didn't think so. The smoothie arrived in a large plastic fountain glass, crowned with a layer of whipped cream. Grant sipped his coffee and watched Sam take long chugs, leaving a foamy mustache on his lip.

"Slow down or you'll get a brain freeze," he warned.

The boy continued to drink with steady determination. "But we should head back soon," Sam said between gulps.

Grant sipped his coffee, almost dumbstruck. His first instinct was to agree — they should go back. Lunch was probably home by now, arms folded as he waited at the dinette, wondering where they were. "I don't think you should go back there anymore," he found himself saying. But whether it was out of concern or jealousy, he did not know.

Sam's brow creased.

We Only Flinch When It Isn't Necessary

"He's not the kind of man you think he is. He's going to hurt you one day and then forget all about you." There were so many reasons he wanted to give him, even though Sam just sat there, becoming more and more expressionless. Grant wanted to tell him about how Lunch had turned him away the previous week. Or the fact that Lunch had been using the church for years to collect young boys like them. And the people Lunch helped evict were probably the ones most likely to recognize that. And it was funny how Lunch was a very religious man in public, but always shed those beliefs behind closed doors. Finally, he wanted to say that the worst kind of holy man was one with influence. But all Grant could do was stutter, unable to piece together a single sentence until he finally said, "You can't trust him. He's like a replicant."

Sam looked deep into the remains of his fountain glass and rapped his fingers against the table top in an agitated fashion. "I don't believe you," Sam said. "You're the meanest person I've ever met."

And then Sam vanished, almost instantly, as if he were a mere figment of Grant's imagination. But as he added more sugar to his coffee, enough so the sweetness made him almost gag, Grant could remember the boy scowling at him, rising from his chair and walking out through the café entrance. It actually happened in slow motion. Grant sat, almost paralyzed in thought, long enough to realize he'd been alone for quite a while. On the other side of the café, the typists worked feverishly at their laptops without looking up. The barista came and quietly took Sam's fountain glass. He could sense her hovering around him, as if ready to say, "We all have to learn these things on our own." But when he turned, she was already at the wash station, dunking coffee mugs in the soapy water.

If she had been there, he would have told her, "I did the best I could," even if it wasn't true. He needed to believe that Sam would turn out fine in the end. After all, there were many boys out there who needed rescuing and most survived without it. He had met one a year ago, back in Boulder. A panhandler had approached him on the street, filthy hand extended. The young man wore what appeared to be the tattered remnants of a prep school uniform. His face was dirty but his hair styled. A gold stud earring caught the light like a glowing star. Grant gave him a dollar and kept walking even though the young man had tried desperately to engage him. "It wasn't supposed to be like this," the panhandler had said. Grant hadn't bothered to find out why. That would take a lot of trust.

Jonathan Harper

No More Heroes

$\mathcal{N}$ow the resort is dark and the bar holds the only signs of life. The gamers crouch around a low table adjacent to the towering slate fireplace. They nurse their drinks and flip their cards. There are five of them: a loud-mouthed group of men in their mid-thirties, who still wear t-shirts with cartoon characters on them, who curse too often and who are lovingly cruel to each other because this is how they perceive the world treats them. With me, there are six of us. (However, over the past few years, I've made it a point to be around less often.)

I order a vodka-cranberry, my second for the night. "Could you make it weak?" I ask. "I don't have much of a tolerance." But the bartender ignores me. Behind us, my group has just unleashed a barrage of obscenities so loud and vulgar that you can't hear anything else. One of my friends has actually used the word "fucktard," which has the same impact as firing off a pistol in a crowded room: stunned silence. The bartender slowly turns back to me. I smile, pretend I haven't heard a thing. "May I please have a vodka-cranberry?" I ask. He hands me a drink that is practically all fruit juice, leans forward and gives me a look that says, "This is a fancy establishment. Settle the fuck down."

The clientele here are a little too upper-class for my taste. They are also territorial, savage and sophisticated, a case study in mob mentality. What my friends don't know is that the patrons have our table surrounded, amphitheater style. They sip their wine, sit cross-legged on their cushioned stools, and they wait. As I make my way back, I can feel their glares like heat on the back of my neck. I wonder if my friends realize how close we are to danger, that at any moment these well-mannered people could turn hostile, grab pitchforks and torches and chase us out into the night.

When Oliver first suggested this trip he had described a cabin in the woods: something rustic, charming and, best of all, secluded. That was the key, he insisted — a long weekend away where we could escape our real lives without interruption. Oliver made all the arrangements, collected our checks in advance. At no point was the resort town mentioned until it was too late. It's preseason November in the mountains and even though the ski slopes aren't open yet the area is saturated with vacationers. The resort itself is cut into the mountainside, full of stone columns and trellises, butcher-block cabins that lie scattered along the ridge, and there's a weather-beaten barn for the resident Shetland ponies. When we first arrived my chest deflated like a balloon as I stared up at the stone manor and thought, *Dear God, we've entered* The Shining.

The card game we are playing is *Creature Coliseum: Battle Royale*, second edition. It's a watered-down version of the fantasy RPGs that have lured nerds into hobby shops for decades. Each player has three hero cards and spends his turn summoning monsters to attack his opponents. Monsters are defeated, treasure cards are drawn and once your heroes are all vanquished you're out. It's a very simple game, very unstrategic: last player standing wins. But we won't delve into the real gaming until later tonight. This is just foreplay.

"Ice troll," Oliver says. He flips over a card with the glossy portrait of a blue-scaled creature and practically throws it in poor Corey's face. "Take two damage, asshat. That'll teach you to fuck with me!"

Corey pouts and discards one of his dead heroes. With each turn we disrupt the bar's tranquility a little more. As I clutch my empty glass, the bartender stares me down, vengefully pours a Drambuie, and I decide I'm really not that thirsty. The gamers continue to heckle each other while the patrons continue to stare and whisper. The army colonel in the corner, the one who has kept his crew cut into retirement, slams his fist on his table. An old constipated-looking woman gnashes her dentures at us with murderous intent. I keep quiet, stay camouflaged under my friends' exhibition, and realize I'm not really that embarrassed. I had all of high school to build up a callus to these sorts of things.

Oliver's on a killing spree. He defeats my Rabid Unicorn, takes two treasure cards and then thrusts a chewed fingernail in poor Corey's direction. "Eat my wrath," he yells and drops a Hell Hound card. "Five damage, fatty," and that kills off Corey's last hero. The gentleman to our left, the one who looks like a well-fed Burt Reynolds, lowers his book and emits a forceful cough.

"Why you always picking on me?" Corey's head drops in mournful surrender. As a teenager he was acne-covered and fat. Now he's nosedived into pure obesity, his body resembling a burlap sack holding mounds of potatoes.

"First one out picks up the tab," Oliver says and folds up the dead hero cards. Oliver is like that. He's embarrassing and a very poor winner. "I rule you, the world, everybody!" He sticks both middle fingers into Corey's face until the bartender yells at him to calm down.

These are my friends and this is the tradition. Every few months the gang gets back together. And even though we are well cemented into adulthood with careers and high cholesterol, some of us with wives and children, all of us touched by our first tragedy (Michael died of a brain tumor right after college), we still reunite to play our games. We are of Generation X but hold the stigma of Generation Y, the generation of me, the mentality that if we do not interact with something, then it does not exist.

I was absorbed into this group during high school. Back then I was the anomaly: the lone queer boy with chunky braces and my own library of fantasy novels. Violent beatings and isolation were the tragedies of gay teenagers. That might have been my fate as well if I had not met Oliver. He had a way of collecting people, usually misfits, ostracized kids with nervous tics and OCD. When he decided to become my friend I felt pulled by the wrist and instantly indoctrinated. At first I didn't care too much for *Dungeons & Dragons*. There were too many rules to learn, too many charts to consult. Everything depended on rolls of weirdly shaped dice and I've never been lucky. But, as Michael explained, the true pleasure wasn't the game itself but the story we shared. It was about the camaraderie of the players. This was why I kept returning to Oliver's basement every weekend, where he ruled as Dungeon Master and we lived in the world he had designed. It was there they gave me a role and I started my second life. I became a cleric.

In most role-playing games there are four basic classifications of characters. My friends are the fighters, wizards and rogues because no one wants to play the cleric. That's a fate similar to floating off into gamer purgatory. Clerics are the most boring characters: they cast healing magic and protective chants, they prefer diplomacy over combat. They never experience the joy of sneaking up on unsuspecting victims and sticking a poisoned dagger into their backs. They aspire to the biblical principle that the meek shall inherit the earth. According to the group this was the job best suited for me, because I myself was so gentle and passive. They gave me weak and clumsy characters, the kind that don't usually survive. Because Oliver saturated his campaigns with epic battles, I was relegated to pathos when I should have been heroic. What was worse, the boys teased me over it constantly. After a month or two I was ready to quit the games altogether until I noticed something. My teammates always protected me. With each new goblin horde or black knight, someone would say, "Guard the cleric," and they would move their pewter figurines around mine in a defensive barrier. In all those years of playing I rarely came to harm. To return the favor, I healed their wounds and blessed their weapons, and together we survived. I believe this was their way of showing that they loved me, that I was a permanent fixture of this group, and in their eyes even the most useless fragile things are sometimes worth protecting.

I have not seen the guys in over six months. While they all stayed within a ten-mile radius of our hometown, I used every available resource to get as far away as possible. While they rooted themselves in lucrative careers, I'd been prancing around academia for the past decade, accumulating master's degrees in sociology and public health, teaching the occasional intro course, still trying to find stability as a researcher without the qualifications of a PhD. In the spring, I leave for Arizona, and will live off a grant while giving health consultations to sex workers and illegal immigrants. It's not an impressive project. There's no salary, just a few thousand dollars to cover four months of living expenses. I won't be helping these people either. I'm going to collect data to assess how much of a burden they are on the free clinics. Funnily enough, since being appointed cleric I had always imagined myself as a sort of healer, that in real life I would somehow save people. However, time has proven that fantasies rarely come true.

$\mathcal{B}$ack at the bar, our card game continues with feverish competition. Our taunts escalate, we attack each other and cheer. Even I get lost in it, smiling brightly, ignoring the glaring patrons. Oliver is a ruthless player but Neil is a tricky card hoarder. He counters every attack against his cards. In the campaigns he only plays wizards. When we need the impossible done, he consults his bag of tricks. In real life Neil is a married accountant with two ADD-riddled boys. He blames his family for every gray hair on his head, even though they showed up in college. Across the table the two Eds clink their rocks glasses together in a silent toast. It is obvious they have formed an alliance. They are an inseparable duo: both are named Ed Jones, both work in IT and both play fighters. For years they've insisted they're identical twins, even though one is short and balding and the other is black.

Meanwhile, poor Corey, who is always the first one to lose, sits quietly to the side playing with his phone.

The game comes to an exciting climax. Oliver and I make a joint strike against the Ed Alliance. Then Neil downs his drink and his eyes widen with glee. He dumps every card in his hand, a grand assault of the fanged and scaly, and obliterates every hero card on the table in one fell swoop. The gamers cheer, the patrons breathe a sigh of relief and Oliver sulks off to order us another round. With the cards put away, the tension in the bar simmers down to normal.

Corey drapes his fleshy arm around my shoulder as if he's leashing a puppy. He says, "I'm glad you're here," for the third time tonight. Out of everyone, Corey is the most starved for affection and kind-hearted to a fault. When we game he plays an evil lady thief who will seduce a man before slitting his throat and looting the corpse. If it were anyone else the guys would take this as an opportunity to question his sexuality. But then, Corey's obesity has reached the point where he's practically genderless and therefore free of the burdens of a more sexual being. "You should come home more often," he adds and I smile at him.

"Yes. We got our asses handed to us last time." Neil sips from his fourth gin and tonic. "Could have used a cleric."

"I'm sorry," I say. "It's not easy to get time off."

Neil gives me an exaggerated nod. "Tell me about it. I had to barter with Sheila up to the last minute to come here." His drink spills as he mimics his wife nagging. He's not drunk but he looks a little off, like the liquor isn't settling well. "By the way, Sheila says hello. She wants you to visit soon. She's got a friend she thinks you'll like."

"No more blind dates," I say. "I can take care of myself in sixty seconds. What do I need someone else for?"

"That's a shame because that guy's been making eyes at you all night," Corey whispers and points to Burt Reynolds in the corner. Burt gives us a flustered look and continues reading.

"Let me give you some advice," Neil slurs. "Don't get married until you're done having sex."

"Then I should have been married a decade ago," Corey says with a moan.

As Neil sways in place, he grows more anxious looking, sucking in deep breaths while sweat bleeds out around his temples. "Dude, you're looking a little green," I tell him. "You're not going to be sick, are you?"

He swallows hard and pushes out a small belch. "Yes. Yes, I am." He puts his drink down and speedwalks to the restroom.

Behind us, Oliver is leaning against the polished bar, speaking to a quartet of middle-aged aristocrats. He leans in dangerously close to one of the women, who clutches her wine glass in an amused pose. She embodies elegance, her hair cropped short, a crème colored shawl guarding her cleavage. "Well, it's nice to see some fresh blood in these parts," she says. The man beside her, probably her husband, sips his whiskey and adds, "A little intimidating, but good!"

"So, are you here for the swinger's party?" Oliver says this a little loud and shoots me a mischievous grin. "Oh, I'm just kidding."

"Do you believe this guy?" the gentleman asks his entourage, who all chuckle uncomfortably.

I cut off poor Corey mid-sentence and point towards Oliver. We wince. "You should probably go get him," Corey says.

My approach is timid. I position myself discreetly at Oliver's back. It takes me only a moment to realize he's attempting to flirt and failing miserably. He flatters the lady with talk of fine wine and social inequality. When she asks how long we are staying, he tells her about our gaming retreats. The woman nods as he explains his role as dungeon master, trying to introduce it in a way that seems like she asked, like it's a matter of prestige and that this should make him exotic. Oliver believes we represent the next wave of the creative elite and, if he can convince this elegant woman, then he can prove it to be true. She's obviously enjoying herself, as poised as a praying mantis, ready to bite off his head.

"There's an artistry to what we do," Oliver tells the woman. "I've been crafting RPG campaigns for years. I'm practically a professional at it."

"I'm sorry, dear. I have no earthly idea what you're talking about."

Tonight, in this bar, we will make ourselves legendary. The bartender leers at Oliver, acts like he's secretly recording the entire conversation. Up close, he's about sixty, face creased into a road map of indentations and scars. When I ask him for a ginger ale, his scowl deepens further. Oliver continues in his vain quest to impress the woman, giving her the physics of creativity, the balance of storytelling and dice mechanics.

"You would get along well with my nephew," she says. "He's fourteen."

I tap Oliver's shoulder and he pulls me in. "This is Richard, our little abortionist." As he laughs, all I smell is the sweet afterthought of liquor on his

breath, and feel the gravitational pull of the woman's eyes. She can smell the sweet afterthought of my discomfort.

"I'm not an abortionist," I manage to say and she nods. "I have a master's in public health." Like that proves something.

"This is Mrs. Tatich. Her husband owns all the local wineries." The look on her face tells me this is also false and somehow that makes us even. "And if I may add, that's such a nice perfume you're wearing."

Mrs. Tatich arches her neck backward, showing off the pale flesh, gives her friends an incredulous look. But before she can respond Neil wanders back, his mouth a little foamy with trace elements of spit up on his collar. He looks like shit. I nod at him to go sit with the others and tell Oliver we need to leave.

"You boys have had enough," the bartender says. "I'll get you your check." The man hates us. It's written all over his face in wrinkles.

"Oh, just charge it to our cabin," Oliver replies, his tone startlingly abrasive, and the bartender slams his register drawer shut. Then Oliver turns back to the woman. "Such a pleasure meeting you. What was your first name?"

"Mrs. Tatich," she says. Her group's laughter is brief but triumphant.

We have officially worn out our welcome.

*O*utside, the chill and rain combine into a feisty tempest. November is known for mood swings. We stumble in the dark towards our cabin at the far side of the resort, the two Eds keeping Neil steady, Corey wobbling along the path like a gelatinous cube. It's a soggy death-defying walk. The path is narrow and one misstep could send a sober man tumbling down into the parking lot below. Somehow we manage. We always have.

What our cabin lacks in rustic charm, it compensates in size. The sitting room has a full table, several clothed couches and a fireplace that lights up with a flick of a switch. The kitchen is roughly the size of my studio apartment. Two full bedrooms and a bunk room, each with a private bath, plenty of space for six men on a weekend getaway. Within an hour we all eat, poop and sober up. The color has returned to Neil's cheeks.

Oliver awaits us at the dinette table. He squats behind his Dungeon Master's screen, a tri-fold cardboard stand with a large mural of adventurers descending into a monster-populated underworld. Behind it are his manuals, charts and notes. He distributes our character sheets and figurines, lays out the map tiles in the center of the table. Our cabin is dimly lit by the fireplace, casting an eerie glow behind Oliver, making him look demonic. His narrow chin is hidden by his folded hands, his widow's peak spikes forward in warning.

"Prepare yourselves," he says. "For a new round of unspeakable horrors awaits you." Oliver makes his coarse voice go as soft as warm mayonnaise. When he takes on the role of Dungeon Master, he likes to believe he is something else, godlike, omniscient, as unbiased as a courtroom judge. While his storytelling has matured over the years, his plots are still the same variety of watered-down epics borrowed from cheap paperback novels. He hates simplistic storylines. No treasure hunts, no dragons. He wants us to believe in consequence. He crafts large-scale adventures about medieval conspiracies and secret societies, and reuses the same plot twists over and over again. But despite all the scripts, I'm sure he makes half of it up as he goes along. Throughout the years, the world has ended twice because of our ineptitude.

"Picking up where we left off, after your embarrassing defeat at the fjord, you've returned to the Inn of Two Dogs to lick your wounds," Oliver says and gives me a wink. "And after his long absence, Brother Randolph rejoins the party." The Inn of Two Dogs is a staple of our games. There's one in every town, perhaps the first-ever fantasy franchise, and after every defeat this is where we return. Our current objective is to meet up with the informant who knows the location of the evil cult we are supposedly fighting against. However, every arranged meeting has been interrupted by an ambush, none of which the gang has won.

"Wait a second," someone says and Oliver glares impatiently. "I thought Randolph was trapped in ice."

"Is that what you did to me?" I ask.

"Yup, he wanted to kill you off, but we wouldn't let him."

"Does it matter?" Oliver snaps and rustles a few papers behind his screen.

"It matters for the sake of continuity."

"Who cares? Let's go back to the fjord and kick some ass."

"He thawed," Oliver mumbles.

"What about the barmaid? Is she hot?" Corey asks.

"Dude, you're playing a chick."

Corey blinks his eyes and smirks. "Oh, right. So, is the bartender hot?"

"I wonder, if you've thawed from a chunk of ice, wouldn't that come with a Constitution penalty?"

Neil belches into his hand, looks like he's suppressing the urge to vomit again. "Maybe we're not supposed to go to the fjord until we've found this informant."

I drink my tea and watch Oliver bang his hand like a gavel. He wants us to concentrate harder and his demands increase every year. To him it's more than a game. It's his own private world, one with serious lessons that we seem uninterested in learning. From behind the screen, the sound of dice clatters against the table and this is what brings the banter to a halt. An assassin dips his knife into my belly. I take damage; I bleed.

"Is this the way you welcome me back?" I ask and meet Oliver's aggressive stare.

"Protect the cleric," the gamers yell, just like old times.

They move their figurines around mine and subdue the assassin but more foes enter. They come in through trapdoors, windows and back rooms; the tavern turns into a battlefield. Our group cleaves them into the afterlife. I heal myself while the hefty bartendress, Gerta, carries out the corpses with the evening garbage. But there is still no sign of the informant, so Corey's lady thief seduces the bartender for information and then backstabs poor Gerta for shits and giggles, so we have to leave the inn in a real hurry.

Another hour passes. We return to the fjord in full force, where an unnatural mist clings to the inlets: a telltale sign of the unholy. The guys have been through this before, but this time we are prepared. When we enter the cultists ambush us, only now I'm here to counteract their curses. Corey's thief takes an arrow in the belly, but instead of her guts spilling out my magic reduces it to a minor flesh wound. I give him a quick high-five and Oliver says, "Don't do that." With the last of the cultists reduced to mounds of meat, the mist clears. There, built into the mountain, is a temple awaiting our investigation.

"How convenient," Neil grumbles. "Shouldn't we go back and find that informant first?"

"Obviously we didn't need to," the Eds say.

"I want to check for traps," Corey insists.

"Seriously, guys, think about this," Neil says. "We're supposed to find this informant first. We have no idea what's in there."

The group debates, restocks on Doritos and Diet Cokes, and debates a little more. And when we get off topic Oliver yells at us to focus, his voice rising to high octaves.

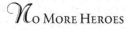

A sudden banging on our cabin door makes us all jump. Corey even yelps. Standing outside is the hefty bartender, the one who hates us, eyes narrowing into evil slits.

"Everyone can hear every damn word you say," he says. All of us line up detention style, averting our eyes, trying to conceal our embarrassed grins. The bartender doesn't wait for an invitation. He stomps inside and slams the windows shut. Who knew they were even open? "Keep it down. People paid good money not to hear you all act like damn fools all night," he says. It's only half past midnight; the hour is still early in gamer-time. But we mutter our apologies and agree to call it a night.

I wake up the next morning spooning Corey, who may or may not be aware of it. In his dreams my body probably belongs to Zooey Deschanel or Ellen Page or some other lithe beauty. I gently slide away as to not interrupt the fantasy. The rest of the cabin is filled with the audible snores of sleeping men. Outside, it's as cold as the breath of winter. Unfortunately I packed poorly for the weekend. Only wearing a pair of drawstring pants and a thermal undershirt with a fleece jacket, I shiver my way out of the door and up to the manor house.

The resort serves a complimentary breakfast to early risers. I arrive in a wood-paneled hearth room on the lower level. Four harvest tables are set up with a buffet of croissants, eggs, bacon and a fruit salad which is mostly cubes of cantaloupe. The other guests greet me with a series of disapproving glances. I'm dressed for a yoga class; they're dressed up for brunch. Thankfully, the Lady Tatich and her entourage are nowhere in sight.

But the Burt Reynolds man is. He sits at the lone table in the corner, brushing flakes of croissant from his mustache while he quietly talks to a bald man in canary-yellow cardigan. I take a seat at the far end, eat oatmeal with raisins, wishing I had a book or my phone or something to distract me. I want nothing more than to be nondescript and non-threatening to the gentle harmony of the hearth room. But the men keep glancing over with expectation until the silence grows awkward enough for me to say, "Good morning," and then add a quick apology for the previous night.

"Well, at least you all bring a little flair," his friend interjects, twiddling his fingers. "These ninnies can afford to have their feathers ruffled once in a while." Perhaps it is the combination of his floating hand gestures and wire-rimmed glasses and his exaggerated eye rolls, but I instantly imagine him

Jonathan Harper

as an artistic director of a theatrical society. He's overly talkative and pulls Burt by the arm to the chairs next to me. I ask them how long they've been together and Burt sighs. "I told you he was on our team," the artistic director says proudly.

When it's my turn to speak I avoid the topic of gaming and instead mention my upcoming research trip, which impresses them enough. They tell me about the resort, how they've been coming here for two decades and know the owners personally.

"There's been a lot of changes over the years," the artistic director whispers. "Twenty years ago this was a queer hideaway."

Burt rolls his eyes. "This place has a sordid past, to put it lightly."

"*Sordid?*" the artistic director gasps. "Back then it was all about free love. They were giving it away for free and so was I!" Apparently where our cabin sits used to be dense woods with walking trails, the kind that lone men would wander at night in hopes of a brief encounter. "You don't even want to know what this room was used for," the artistic director says and then reminds me to finish up my oatmeal.

By the time the gamers arrive it's nearly ten and the hearth room is emptying out, the buffet depleted except for crumbs and derelict pieces of fruit. Of course Oliver starts to complain and an attendant politely informs him that the restaurant will open at lunchtime.

*C*orey and I take a short walk around the property and an hour passes quickly. Time is stealthy here. We walk down the slope away from the manor house to the edge of the wooden fence, long grayed with age, and I am tempted to freak him out. I want to say that we're walking on sacred ground, that this was a place of wild gay orgies that time forgot. Instead, we stop to admire one of the Shetland ponies, a fat yellow monster who watches Corey toss an apple from hand to hand. A posted sign warns us: the pony is cute but he bites.

"Oliver's been a real dick lately." Corey says this in a low deadpan voice. "Acted like he was gunning for me all night. It's like he's desperate to kill me off."

I shrug my shoulders. I don't want to feed Corey's sensitivities. "He's always been difficult," I say.

"Yeah, well, he got us in trouble last night. He charged the tab to our cabin and didn't leave a tip for the bartender, which explains why the guy barged in on us. When I told him this morning, he said it was my fault for not paying the tab and now he's ignoring me."

"I don't understand. Why is that your fault?"

As Corey grunts, his entire body vibrates a little. "I was the first one out, remember? Oliver randomly decided that meant I pay the tab."

I shuffle in place for a few moments, thinking back to the days right after Michael died, when just the three of us would convene at the old apartment for all-night movie fests. Oliver, the master of the art of Japanese cooking, would serve us shabu-shabu and sushi rolls. We'd force ourselves to stay awake as if we dreaded the idea of morning. And then I realize that was ten years ago.

"Look, Oliver picks on you because you're a gentleman. He knows you won't push back."

Corey gives me a sad look. "A month ago he showed us some weird internet video and I said it frightened and confused me. I thought I was being humorous. The next day, he emails me this long-ass manifesto telling me that I overuse the phrase and it has insulting undertones. I was stumped. So I asked him, what's the big deal? He says similar shit all the time. This gets me an even longer rebuttal where he lists a dozen things I don't remember saying and how he tolerates me because I have no other friends. What do you say to that?"

"I bet there was something else going on. He was probably taking his anger out on you."

"Well, it gets worse. Oliver didn't speak to me for the rest of the month and then called me a few days ago saying he still needed my share for this trip." Corey holds out the apple and beckons the pony. It stares back at us with vacant confusion. "So, I told him I didn't think I was still invited and then he started yelling at me and calling me an attention-seeker. He almost made me cry. Imagine me, a grown man, crying over this bullshit."

We idle a bit longer, the Shetland remaining out of arm's reach. We have all heard rumors that Oliver takes medicine for his mood swings. But it's a topic he guards well. Corey tells me that Oliver lost his job again, that besides the gaming nights he rarely sees anybody.

"Jesus, I didn't know things were that bad," I say.

"You should come home more often."

A sudden chill makes me pull my fleece tighter. "How is he even paying for this?"

"Unemployment, probably. He's spent a good year isolating himself, hoarding his savings and rationalizing being angry at everyone. Sometimes I think he's just given up. What do you think?"

"I think we spend too much time talking about Oliver," I say.

Corey nods, but I know he's disappointed in me. He returns his attention to the blonde pony. "Do you want the apple or not?" he barks and lobs it underhand. The apple smacks against the creature's side and rolls off into the wet grass.

"Don't you hurt her," comes a shrill voice from behind us. Two small girls, both in matching pink coats, glare at us with the horrified O's of their gaping mouths. "You're horrible," screams the other girl and both run back to the lodge calling out for their mother. By the time I turn around Corey is running off in the opposite direction, his feet stumbling on the slope until he falls backward like a crashing blimp. It's the saddest-funniest thing I've ever seen. But considering our growing reputation, abusing the Shetlands could be the final straw and I'd hate another confrontation with the bartender. I take off running as well.

*A*t noon we reconvene in the manor house's game room, a large rectangular space decorated like some gentleman's club from a past era. A billiards table stands in the back next to an old-fashioned dartboard and a cluster of leather sofas. Antique Persian rugs cover the floorboards. Oliver is waiting on us, his mouth drooping in an impatient frown. On a claw-footed card table, he's set up his Dungeon Master's screen and tile maps. On the nearby buffet sits our nerd brunch of Cheetos and Diet Coke.

"Wouldn't we feel more comfortable back in the cabin?" I suggest but Oliver shakes his head.

"Why? There's more space here," he says. "We're paying for ambiance and this is it."

Corey shuffles in his place. "I don't want to feel like we're on display."

Oliver tells us to shut up, that we're staying put. Besides, the resort is practically empty. Most of the guests are in town windowshopping or at the nearby horse farms for riding lessons. The handful of stragglers left are either in the bar for an early-afternoon cocktail or locked away in the reading room on the main floor. Maybe somewhere a couple is having middle-aged sex in their cabin. Who knows? Currently, it's only us and the game room, our manuals, dice and enough soda to kill lab rats. Neil even produces a bottle of rum because we're on vacation and deserve it.

"Before we begin, I have an announcement to make," Oliver says as we take our seats at our very own Round Table. "Today is the final chapter of your saga. Whatever happens, this is the end. Point being, I've painstakingly crafted this epic for over three years and because of your ADD and negligence to detail you've made pathetic progress. And I won't put up with it anymore." Oliver pauses to fix himself a drink, a healthy dose of rum, and he raises his red plastic cup like a king's goblet. "It's time to move on. From this point forward, character death is permanent. No resurrection." He gives me an authoritative nod. "The decisions you make today will determine not only the basis of my next campaign but the future of this group."

We all exchange glances of disbelief, like we're looking for permission to be offended. Corey's face is full of alarm, probably wondering if Oliver would instantly kill him off. At this point his thief could drop dead from any number of venereal diseases.

"That doesn't sound fair," Ed grumbles and Ed nods in agreement.

But Oliver shrugs his boney shoulders, his eyes growing feral. "We all must suffer the consequences of the choices we make."

"I cast *Cure Disease* on Corey," I say. "Just to be safe."

We pick up at the fjord and continue into the ruins. We battle cultists and ghouls, find a meager amount of treasure. Stirges and vampire bats lurk throughout the interior chambers. At the very end is an imprisoned scribe, an angry old man who berates us for not coming to his rescue sooner. He tells us to return to the Inn of Two Dogs, that our faithful resting place is actually the source of all our troubles. Underneath it lies the breeding ground for evil and Gerta, the husky bartendress Corey murdered, had been our informant all along. The scribe continues to chastise us until Corey backstabs him. Everyone applauds. As we trace our way back to town, I ask to stop at my cleric's temple to record our travels with the historians.

"If we fail, someone should know where to pick up where we left off."

For the first time in what feels like years, Oliver gives an approving smile.

At the inn, the patrons and bartender attack, which seems oddly appropriate, and we slaughter them like helpless cattle. Our team boasts with overconfidence. It's Corey who discovers the hidden door in the wine cellar that leads us to a candlelit chamber holding a tainted altar. I purify it and that opens a passage into the catacombs below. It is a simple dungeon, full of shackled

Jonathan Harper

skeletons and green slime, cryptic writing etched into stone walls. We lose our first player in the tombs. While trying to cast a spell, Neil's wizard gets knocked back into a pit of flesh-eating beetles and is instantly devoured.

"Fucking hell," he snaps. "When the fuck did you idiots forget to watch my back?" But as Neil starts rolling up a new character, our Dungeon Master shakes his head.

"There's no need for that," Oliver says. "I told you. This is the end."

"What am I supposed to do now?"

"You're dead, dude. Go get a beer and sit quietly. This will be over soon."

"Fuck off, you tyrant," Neil replies and pours himself another rum and Coke.

Soon our card table is covered with little tile pieces, a long winding maze full of dead rats and bones. When we reach its end, we make a deal with a demon and it informs us that our final enemy is the village itself, that while we had worked so hard to protect it we had failed to notice its growing corruption. The demon taunts us, it cackles. It gives us a scroll, the parchment made of human flesh. All we need to do is read it in the center of town and that will banish all evil. Of course, demons can never be trusted. But this is the end, which means there's no room for one of Oliver's notorious plot twists. There's no more incentive to extend the game. We will either read the scroll and win or die trying.

We retrace our steps through the catacombs and ascend back to the surface. And there, in the Inn of Two Dogs, the reanimated corpse of Gerta slaughters Ed's fighter.

We pause as two bourgeois men with sweaty faces walk into the game room. They have obviously come from the bar downstairs, holding their drinks and glancing over at us with mild amusement as they set up the billiards table. With every crack of the cue ball Oliver visibly shudders, giving the men annoyed glares. They ignore us.

Our three surviving heroes creep through the village towards the town square. Walking corpses rise from the graveyard. Possessed villagers come rushing out of their cottages. Even the shadows claw at our heels. Ed's virtuous paladin is the next to fall. He sacrifices himself to the encroaching horde to buy us more time.

"That was very noble of you," Oliver tells him.

"Thanks. Maybe they'll write songs about me later."

"I won't," the other Ed adds and hands him a plastic cup.

Our three deceased sit quietly on the side and drink. Only Corey and I remain, the vixen and the acolyte. We take the demon scroll to the town square as we were instructed. Because Neil's wizard is dead, my cleric is the only one left who can read it. A legion of undead villagers and cultists awaits us, scythes drawn, wanting to drink our blood and bathe in our guts.

Oliver hands me a sheet of paper. "All you got to do is recite the scroll and you save the village," he says. The page is full of nonsensical words, each handwritten and nearly illegible. "Read it out loud," he instructs. "Mess up and you got to start over."

"Nice knowing you, Brother Randolph," Corey says. His thief draws her two daggers and prepares to fend off the horde. It is not a fair fight without our friends, but that's the way Oliver planned it. I start to read, 'Urgst Nefullen Alg *Cunt*…' and then I stop. The two billiards players look over, eyebrows cocked. Everyone is quiet. My eyes trace over a dozen words scattered in the text. *Nigger*. *Faggotfucker*. "What the hell is this?" I stammer.

"Uh-oh. Looks like you have to begin again." Oliver rolls his die and Corey takes an arrow in the boob.

Another quick glance at the paper reveals a dozen more obscenities. I do not like conflict. For years others had fought my battles for me. But Oliver's sadistic grin looks like a challenge. I will my face into a look of indifference and crumple up the paper. "You've crossed a line. I'm not reading this."

More dice roll. "I expected more of you," Oliver says.

"Come on, buddy. All you got to do is believe in yourself," one of the pool players calls out. The two men stand shoulder to shoulder, almost bridged into one. "The world is counting on you," the other one adds and gives me a drunken salute with his rocks glass.

In this moment all eyes are on me. No one knows what is written on the page and I do not know what to say or if I should just walk out of the room. Thankfully I don't have to do either. Corey's phone suddenly rings.

"It's the office," he says and huffs out of his chair with visible relief.

"What the fuck are you doing, fat ass?" Oliver yells this so loudly I flinch. But Corey flaps his hand at him and walks off to the corner wall with the picture window, talking tech speak into his phone. Oliver looks incredulous. His teeth start grinding as his face turns bright red. "Get off the fucking phone." He lets his anger pour out like smog. The two billiards players shoot each other wide-eyed grins. I'm even smiling, compulsively, because I'm not sure if this is all some big joke.

"Leave him alone," Neil says.

"We promised to get away from all that." Oliver stabs his finger forward like an accusation. "No work, no distractions. I needed this," he says and when I try to intervene, my voice fades into a whisper.

It's Neil who steps forward. "Be quiet. He has a job. You remember what that's like, right?"

Everyone freezes; Corey's rambling phone call blends into background noise. And then whatever clockwork exists in Oliver's mind winds up in full force and he begins shouting, nonsensically at first. He asks what the fuck is wrong with us. He shoots out proclamations of wasted time and energy, his true work and worthless friendships. For a moment he seems ready to pounce, claws out, for Neil's throat. It's our silence that probably hurts him. Then Oliver swipes his hand across the table, knocking over his screen and several plastic cups. Rum and Coke spread over his notes, the game tiles and down onto the rug. The two billiards players have stopped laughing and both make a quick exit. Oliver just stands there, watching his expensive game manuals soak up the dark liquids, and then stomps out of the room.

In the corner Corey murmurs a last few words into his phone. I only make out a few of them: an alarm has gone off in one of his buildings and he's giving instructions. The others mill around, fidgeting. By the time I return with a roll of toilet paper from the washroom, the bartender is blotting the carpet.

"I'm so sorry about this," I try to tell him but he orders us out.

It is already dinner time and we can't find Oliver anywhere. Without him, we try our luck at the resort's restaurant but are denied entry by a blonde hostess who keeps her elbows bent at rigid sharp angles. She reminds me of my sister's old Barbie dolls with her vacant eyes and a smile that looks painted onto her face. She is flanked by a pair of waiters, the kind of bodyguards that will kick your ass before offering you a dessert menu. The hostess explains that reservations are required and there's a dress code, too. "I'm sorry. We can't accommodate you tonight," she says, even though most of the tables are empty.

Thankfully, Corey's mild-mannered enough not to argue. "Never mind then," he tells her. "There's a Waffle House down the road. At least there, you're always overdressed."

The guys go out to the cars and drive off towards town, but I stay behind. It's a glorious night to spend on the open grounds, the sky blossoming pink and purple, shadows dancing over the stone walkways. We all need some time alone. Another casual walk around the property, passing the Shetland pony and the barn, and I fall into a little fantasy that Burt Reynolds and the artistic director will stumble upon me and invite me to dinner. Then we'll sit in the bar for a glass of wine, perhaps move to their room for a late-night chat. Of course, this doesn't happen and the air turns chilly. Soon it's too cold to loiter outside.

When I arrive back at the cabin, I find Oliver pacing around in circles. He gives off the impression of a pulsing ball of electricity ready to combust. I ask if he's all right. He shrugs and asks, "Where are the others?"

"They went to find food."

"Figures," he says with a roll of his eyes. "But I'm glad it's just you. I want to show you something. Grab a towel. If you don't have swim trunks, I'll loan you mine."

I don't move.

"Oh come on," he says. "We were playing. Shit happens."

"Games are supposed to be fun. That wasn't."

Oliver looks agitated, like I'm misunderstanding him, like I'm being difficult on purpose. He fumbles through an explanation but doesn't offer an apology. I've never understood people who rationalize away bad behavior. If Michael were here, if he were still alive, none of this would have happened. Michael was a true peacemaker. He could solve an argument before it even started. Me, I'm too passive to intervene. I've always relied on flight over fight. I'm not a diplomat like Michael and, with him gone, there's no one here to maintain that balance. For years we've kept on playing without a central character. And at this point what purpose does our game serve except allow us to continue existing in each other's company without ever having to really talk to each other?

"Fine," I say and Oliver's face relaxes. He even smiles.

Oliver leads me down towards the manor house and we pass under the wooden archway to the stone-cut patio. The pool is closed for the winter, covered with a brown foam mat. An iron circular staircase leads up to the back entrance of the bar. Hidden underneath the stairs sits a pair of engraved French doors that Oliver pulls open, releasing a sudden blast of warm humidity. The chamber within is decorated like an enchanted grotto with dozens

 *Jonathan Harper*

of fake green plants and stones surrounding a large hot tub. It's like a buried treasure. You wouldn't know to look for it.

"Alone at last," he says. I wear his trunks and he's naked and neck deep in the bubbling cauldron. His pale body is much thinner and hairier than I expected.

"You know the guys are pissed off at you," I say and avert my gaze so he won't think I'm trying to nab a glimpse of his penis.

"Them or you?" he asks while spinning around the center of the tub. His furry butt is visible under the water.

I want to tell him so many things, like I'm sorry that I don't respond to his emails or that I can't live in the same suburban pit all my life. I want him to understand that the quirks that distinguish us when we are young do not always carry over well into adulthood. Instead, I say, "Yes. I'm upset right now."

"Richard, I don't know why I wrote that scroll up. I guess I wanted to see your reaction. I went a little overboard and I'm sorry, but we should move on." I tell him I'm worried, that I've heard stories. Oliver doesn't share my concern. "Truth is, no — I do not take medicine and I find it insulting when people say I should. Yes, I lost my job because my boss hated me. And because you're not here, you don't know what it's like to be stuck with those assholes. They use me to escape their own pathetic lives yet they're constantly telling me what I do wrong with mine. I hate them so much, it gnaws at me."

We sit and stew and remain quiet for several minutes. The water is too hot and I need to take breaks. "I wonder if you're scared they're outgrowing you and that what you have to contribute isn't important anymore." As I say this, Oliver shakes his head with a half-grin, acting like I don't understand anything. "Listen carefully," I tell him. "We didn't come out here just to role-play. We came here for you. But this isn't high school anymore. You're not the leader. And poor Corey, you need to be kinder to him. There's a lot more to him then you give him credit for."

"Corey." He says the name like it's pitiful.

"Yes, Corey. He's a hard worker and a good friend and if you don't take care of him he is going to move on."

After a short pause, Oliver forces another smile. "You were always my favorite, Richard. You actually got out and did something with your life."

"No, I haven't."

The hot tub's timer buzzes and the bubbles stop. In the clear water, I see his full body and the wavering image of his penis. It is the closest to intimacy I've experienced in months. Oliver flings himself over the edge, the two half-moons of his butt in full view, turns the dial and the water jets start again.

"You're running off to Arizona on your great expedition," he says. "Meanwhile, I'm stuck at the loser's table."

"Be nice."

"This isn't really about them. It is, but it isn't. I don't want to end up like them, rotting away in some cubicle and waiting for something to happen. That's not genuine living. There's no creation in it. They don't think or read or have opinions. They just do maintenance. That's not what I'm meant for."

I tell him I don't understand his point. Now he gets cocky.

"You're not hearing me right. What's good enough for them isn't what's good enough for me. Gaming isn't just a recreational sport anymore — it's a way of life. It's an industry!" He slaps his hands against the water. "The real reason I brought you here is because I have an idea and I want your advice. The industry is making a comeback. Let that marinate a moment. I could own a store and use that to fund my own gaming modules. I've got years worth of materials and the ideas just keep coming. Every single time this group gets together, I transcribe that shit, from every in-game decision to every time people lose focus. I got the psychiatry down for this."

"Sounds impressive. What are you going to do with all that?"

"Well, you're the researcher. What do you do with raw data? All I know is that I have enough information logged away for a ten-book series. With a little help, I could do something with this. Start a franchise, even."

My brow creases. I glance at the absurdity of the plastic leaves drooping over the tub. Little beads of chlorinated water drip off them.

"I need an investor." He says this in a professional-grade calming voice as I instinctively shake my head. "You got this big-deal grant, right? How much money did they give you?"

"Not enough."

"Well, what is it? Twenty thousand? Fifteen? How many abortions will that pay for?"

A pang of disgust hits me like a dozen needles jabbing my stomach. Somewhere, Corey and the guys are sitting together over a hot meal, laughing at some inside joke that no one around will understand. I wish I had gone with them. I wish I just stayed home.

Jonathan Harper

"Now you're mad at me." Oliver pats my shoulder in condescending fashion. "I was just teasing," he says and glides forward, a little too close, and I feel his junk brush against my knee. "You're one of my oldest friends. No one else takes me seriously like you do. All I need is a little guidance and a loan, that's all."

The French doors open, letting in a breath of cold, and in walks Burt Reynolds and the artistic director, both wearing oversized robes with towels slung over their shoulders. One of them lets out a prissy chirp, obviously delighted to see Oliver leaning over me with the ridge of his naked ass eclipsing the water.

"Are we interrupting something?" Burt asks, twitching his mustache.

"No. You aren't," I say. The heat swells again. I feel short of breath but I have an erection and can't risk standing up.

"How disappointing," says the artistic director. "For a moment it felt like the good old days."

Oliver laughs to himself and glides away, steps out of the tub with his penis in full view, drooping like a soggy corsage. He blots himself dry while the two men share conspiratorial glances. When Oliver is dressed, he calmly walks out of the grotto. "He's all yours, boys," he calls back and leaves me alone with the two gawking queens.

      I don't see Oliver for the rest of the night. I don't go back to the cabin to change. Instead, I call Corey and ask him to come pick me up. It takes him nearly twenty minutes to drive up to the resort while I wait outside in the cold, using the damp towel as a cloak. When his sedan comes wheezing along the gravel road, he does not ask what's happened or where I've been, even when it's obvious that my wet trunks are bleeding through my pants and onto his leather seats. Only once does he turn and ask, "Is everything all right?" I shiver and stare out of the passenger window.

"It is now," I tell him.

After a short drive, we pull into a dive-bar pizzeria. The establishment has a dark grim feel, dirty floors and vulgar hearts, neither restaurant nor bar, but a simple waiting room disguised as both. Places like this have a real allure for the downtrodden and underprivileged, those not welcome in the resorts. And perhaps to those trying to escape them.

The guys sit in an oversized booth, already too deep in discussion to notice our arrival. They are debating which anime film is better: the original 1970s

Vampire Hunter D or the more recent sequel, *Vampire Hunter D: Blood Lust*. I simply roll my eyes; the debate is asinine. It is universally accepted that the original is the better film even if the sequel has superior animation. I feed a dollar to the jukebox and order curly fries, which come out as a steamy starchy plate of goodness. And while there are no cultist conspiracies to unravel or dungeons to explore, there is a contagious laughter. Every vapid statement I hear possesses a joyous ring of authenticity. Suddenly Corey is nudging me and he tells everyone about our dangerous encounter with the Shetland pony and the two screaming girls who threatened to report us to the authorities. In another booth, I spy a group of teenagers, huddled together in their hooded jackets, laughing, and there amongst them is the lone fey boy, buckled in place with a patient grin.

We outlast the rest of the customers, multiple pitchers deep, all the way to last call. The hefty waiters are stacking chairs on the tabletops by the time we settle our tab. The drive back is vaguely treacherous, all of us a little tipsy and anxious, but somehow we arrive at our cabin on the far side of the hill. We sluggishly collapse into chairs and couches with a little talk of a card game before bed. And we all notice it, even though nobody acknowledges it aloud. Oliver's bed is empty and his suitcase is gone.

Nobody gives a shit.

*B*y mid-morning our bags are packed and the cabin is clean enough. Even though we prepaid for a third night, the decision to leave early is unanimous. As a group, we march down to deposit the keys in the resort office. There, a sharp-nosed man with freckles stands with an expectant look on his face. He prints our bill with a vengeance. "Three nights and the bar tabs. Your total due is at the bottom."

"We prepaid," Corey says and the attendant sucks in air through his teeth before pressing a few keys on his computer. I tug Corey's sleeve and tell him I sent my check to Oliver over a month ago. We all had, of course.

The attendant attacks his keyboard. "No prepayment was made," he says. We stare dumbly at him in a discombobulated clump. It's Corey who summons enough melancholic dignity to hand over his credit card and ushers us out.

*O*ur caravan doesn't make it far. Corey's sedan leads the way, traversing the narrow lanes of the mountains where the trees grow barren,

the last of their browned leaves clinging to stark branches. As I stare out into the hills, mentally drifting, I find myself talking about a haunted feeling, like we're escaping a wasteland.

Just before the highway we pull into a roadside diner, a cheap one with red-checkered table clothes and a chrome counter. Six of us, minus one, and there's the depressing thought that long ago we had been seven. The crusty old waitress tosses our menus in the center of the table. "Where you hons all comin' from?" she asks and flashes us her grisly teeth. We give each other disgruntled looks. We act tired and miserable. Except Corey. He gives her a polite smile, gives her a pleasant version of our weekend before encouraging us to make our orders. The waitress ignores our moodiness and brings us an orange juice pitcher, coffee and rubbery omelets before she goes outside to smoke. Otherwise the diner is empty.

As we pick at our food, Corey lays out the lodging receipt in front of him. For the first time ever he looks confident, almost assertive. "So we were in the most expensive cabin. We have the unpaid bar tab and apparently Oliver added another one last night. Gratuity was added because no one bothered to tip. And there's a cleaning charge for the rug we ruined. It all breaks down to a little over $300 per person."

"Does that include Oliver's share?" I ask.

Corey shakes his head and his thick neck jiggles. "Don't be foolish. We're not getting any money out of him."

"This is too much," Ed says and Ed adds, "This whole trip was his idea."

Neil shakes his head. "I already paid him. Sheila's going to kill me if I have to shell out another three hundred."

I feel my chest buckle; it's difficult to breath. "I can't afford this," I cry out and everyone shoots me agitated glares.

"Are you serious?" Neil snaps. "We all got screwed here, not just you."

"You don't understand," I tell them. "I don't have a regular salary. I don't even have health insurance. Every penny is budgeted — how am I supposed to eat?" And at this moment, all I can see are the months ahead of ramen noodles and an unpaid credit-card bill, counting down the days until my grant check arrives in the mail. Then I feel a warmth cup my shoulder and Corey gives me a quick but tight man-hug. The Eds say they'll help cover my share and Neil calls Oliver a bastard under his breath. "Please ignore me," I say. "I can contribute. It's just stressful. That's all."

$\mathcal{N}$o More Heroes

Outside, snow flurries begin to fall. It feels like a premonition. "You all want the check, hons?" the waitress asks and we nod. But we stay seated, watching the snow, juggling our wallets and raiding the surrounding tables for more sugar packets. We put a good hour behind us bashing Oliver's name, recounting his failures and the favors he still owes us. But we are afraid to leave the diner. It's an act too heavy with finality. It was something we'd never considered before: what happens to the heroes when the quest is over? What if all we have left are a few scattered memories of the surreal and fantastic? Remember that time when Michael jumped off the cliff and then tried drinking his potion of "feather fall"? Or what about the four-breasted succubus in the Tower of Dread — that was pretty funny. Oh, and when those gnome children we rescued turned out to be werewolves?

"Come on, guys," Corey says with a chuckle. "Let's find something else to talk about."

But there is nothing else, no matter how hard we try to think of a topic.

Wallflowers

The house was a phony, a fraud, a fake. It was tucked away on the far side of Cavalier Park near the old abandoned post office. Why anyone would choose to build in this part of town we did not know. In comparison to our homes it was far too big and gaudy, a pretentious mix of stone and wood. The gardens were full of red plastic flowers that bobbed gently as we touched them; the front door was painted black like a gaping mouth. We had only come to see it because summer break was ending, our freedom slipping away, and it was the only place left to explore.

"A Craftsman," Margot called it. She was the new girl. Her daddy was a builder and had moved to this side of the Chesapeake Bay to bring great changes. We didn't know what that meant. To us the town of Henderson was already a sunken ship. Each year it got smaller. Not in size, but in mentality. It was falling into disrepair, its good citizens getting too fat and complacent. They liked tradition and church and most of all, the unambiguous. None of them knew where we were that afternoon. Nor did they care to know that change was coming.

Margot kept a brass key tied around her neck. She claimed she had one for every house her father built. She led us through the garage, still just a skeleton of wood beams and a plastic canopy nailed on top, and jimmied open the back door. Inside were the bare bones of an unfinished project: blank drywall, exposed pipes and wires; the kitchen cabinets were still stacked in the corner awaiting assembly. Thankfully, we discovered the toilet didn't flush before we regretted using it. As we wandered the first floor our footsteps echoed. We left hand prints on the walls, picked at the loose tiles of the fireplace, kicked open doors, searched every crevice even if we didn't know what we were looking for. What we wanted was a mystery or a haunting. But what we got was just a house, as lame as anywhere else in Henderson. We realized it must be abandoned for a reason. We had no business being there. So we left, a little disgruntled, barely giving Margot enough time to lock up behind us.

"Carpe diem," Mrs. Burkett said and wrote it on the chalkboard. "Can anyone tell me what this means?"

Our first day in Henderson High School ended in Latin class. We had no interest in dead languages. The latest trend in school electives was the cinema studies class, where students sat in a dark auditorium and pretended to watch films. Latin, with so many empty seats, was the safer choice for students like us.

"Carpe diem means 'seize the day.' It's a very common expression." Mrs. Burkett's hair was jet black with a thick gray streak. She wore dark lacy dresses and looked like an undead princess. We liked her. "Say it with me: Carpe diem!" Her face beamed with enthusiasm but again, we didn't answer. "Come on, now. There's no place for wallflowers in this class."

Funnily enough, we had never heard that word before, but instantly knew what it meant. We were wallflowers. Scarred, ugly, odd and untalented, we rarely spoke, never participated. We were all acutely aware that while the adult world mostly ignored us, the young were in the habit of attacking their weak.

"One more try, class. *Carpe diem*," she commanded.

A voice came from the back row. "Carpe scrotum!" and Benny Robertson erupted into self-congratulatory laughter. No one liked Benny, not even us. "Get it? Seize the balls!"

"That was very clever," Mrs. Burkett said and escorted him out to the hall. This was why Benny was left out of our plans. He was too loud, too vulgar, too starved for attention. Wallflowers were calm, dignified. We knew how to disappear.

We returned to the house simply because we could, but mostly because we had nowhere else to go. We were so bored, so boring, waiting for something to happen. This was the peril of our age, no more than fourteen: scornful of adulthood, offended by the mundane. We had orphan fantasies; we wanted to feel transformed. And worst of all, we were terribly self-conscious about it.

It was Margot who invented our games. She was willing to do anything to keep us from being quiet. She would start with a name, one picked at random, and we were asked to fill in the details. The goal was to cause discomfort and laughter. We described them in ugly detail, gave them dirty habits

Jonathan Harper

and addictions. We took turns inventing their lives, these shameful lists of mishaps and failures, always leading to their demise. The death scenes we created were far better than any horror film. Without realizing it, we had soon created an entire community of imaginary misfits, the old tenants of the house, and began writing their histories upon the walls until the every bit of white space was covered.

None of us could recall how Jonas was created. Some blamed Mrs. Burkett's strange lessons. "Household deities," she said. "Di tenante." She taught as if we sat around a campfire swapping ghost stories. Lares, spirits that hovered over places, protectors of the hearth and home. This was a lesson that stuck. If we wanted a haunting, we'd have to do it ourselves.

Margot was the first to really evoke the name. "Jonas," she said and let it echo throughout the house. We uttered it like a dare, as if it tickled, as if Jonas were some ghoulish apparition who threatened to appear if we called him too many times. We wandered the house searching for him, from the concrete basement to the empty rooms on the upper floor. We began to greet him as we entered the house each afternoon. He became the center of all our games. We told him our secrets, our revenge fantasies, as if he was standing there amongst us. And when his name appeared in scrawled letters above the fireplace, we nodded to each other with approval.

In Latin class, the words "Carpe Scrotum" appeared on the chalkboard. Mrs. Burkett came waltzing in, tardy as usual, and observed the letters with cautious amusement. "All right, who wrote this?" she half-sang. Someone whispered, "Jonas," and the classroom filled with hideous laughter. We watched quietly as she escorted Benny Robertson out of the room. The entire hallway could hear him protest. This happened only once.

$\mathcal{A}$ month passed and our parents grew suspicious. They watched us enter well after dark, their eyes darting between us and the clock. They were curious but not concerned. Henderson was still a small town without much trouble and we were not the types to cause any. The evenings continued on as normal: in front of television sets, our families hovered over their dinner trays, always struggling for something to talk about. When they finally asked what kept us out so late, we told them we were out with Jonas and did our best not to grin.

$\mathcal{W}$e all agreed, Jonas was the best thing to happen to us and could not remember what life was like without him. He gave us permission to talk freely, to think aloud. He gave us a sense of purpose. Even if we couldn't remember what we specifically did each afternoon, we basked in the glory of our endless laughter. While in the house we were insulated from the outside world, its cruel mechanisms, its falsehood, and the more we knew we were better off alone.

Then the "No Trespassing" sign appeared and everything shattered. We stood there, dumbstruck, looking at the heavy block letters. Perhaps we had grown too comfortable with the emptiness of the park and the boarded-up post office. It no longer occurred to us that we were trespassers. But Margot still had her key and coaxed us inside. Our graffiti was painted over, the kitchen cabinets restacked, the loose tiles of the fireplace removed. Every mark we'd left had been erased and yet, even in all that emptiness, there was a terrible sensation we were being watched.

We didn't return after that, no matter how much Margot begged. She'd flash her key in the middle of class or stalk us to our lockers. "This changes nothing," she said. To us, our time together had been fun, but now we felt depleted — as hollowed out as the empty rooms. The games were over and it was time to move on. None of us said this to Margot. She was turning possessive and hysterical. One day she gave a long rambling speech about reclaiming what was ours. She shoved us roughly, demanding not to be ignored. And when we still said nothing she slapped her fists against her bag and stomped off towards the park alone. What she did out there all by herself we could not imagine. It was the first time we wondered if there was something seriously wrong with her.

Instead we tried meeting in our own homes, a different one each afternoon. The problem was our parents. As soon as we came through the front door they openly stared, almost horrified by the size of our group. They could not comprehend where we all had come from or what we wanted. All we wanted was privacy: soundproofed walls and dimly lit spaces. We wanted to feel abandoned. While our parents barely spoke, they still hovered in the periphery. Sometimes they brought us little offerings of cookies and soda cans. Other times we caught them peering around the doorways, staring in bewilderment before they rushed away when we turned to face them.

$\mathcal{O}$utside of Latin class we barely saw each other.

$\mathcal{H}$alloween approached and the high school exploded with paper ghosts and foam gravestones. A gallery of jack-o'-lanterns grinned in the front office. Mrs. Burkett wore a black witch's hat for a week and cast spells over the Latin texts. Benny Robertson continued to interrupt class with his embarrassing outbursts. Every time he spoke we rolled our eyes. We'd begun to accept the new routine, waiting for each day to end so we could go home and dread the next. But Margot broke her silence. She whispered that her father planned to resume construction on the house and dangled her key. Then all we could think about was our boredom and our desire for one last gathering. When you are young and neglected you don't just kill time, you slay it dead.

Halloween seemed like a night for last chances. Even the students in film class knew that. We waited for the sun to set, ate lukewarm dinners and donned our silly costumes. Across the park, we marched to the house, which had grown even more rundown in our absence. Margot unlocked the back door and we each muttered "Hello, Jonas" as we passed through. The stale air reeked with the smell of paint. In the foyer we sat cross-legged, our flashlights cutting the dark, as we struggled to remember the old games. Mostly we waited. One of us had stolen a bottle of vodka from his father's study. It circulated a second time, then a third, our lips puckering at the astringent taste. Somehow we were back at the beginning, morose and fuzzy-headed and a little relieved when Margot took a boy upstairs.

We only meant to stay an hour but we got lost in trying to prolong the moment. It was pitch black outside, far later than we'd ever stayed out before. And then we heard the siren as the windows illuminated with blue and red lights. None of this surprised us — we had been expecting it. When the front door opened the police officer peered inside, a hand on his holstered gun. He was surprised to find us lined up patiently waiting for him.

Outside we were presented to a large man with tattoo sleeves. He stood with his arms crossed, his mouth contorted into a monstrous sneer. We had never seen him before but we knew who he was. Margot stepped forward. "Hi, Daddy," she said with nothing but crude indifference. Her father didn't flinch. He grabbed her by the arm, pulled her into his car and drove off, leaving the policeman speechless.

Our parents were summoned, bringing with them that confused apathy we had grown to detest. They could not seem to grasp the situation and stared blankly as the officer said the owners would not press charges, that we were free to go with a warning. For this we were grateful. We moved towards the cars, thinking we could put this awful night behind us.

But instead, one parent asked, "Which one of you is Jonas?"

We looked at one another but said nothing.

"These are the only kids I found," the officer told them. But our parents insisted there was one more child not accounted for. "You mean the girl? Her father took her home," the officer said.

"No. There's a boy. Jonas." Our parents tried describing him, each having heard so little but confident they knew enough. Together they fumbled through a generic description, no one willing to contradict what was previously said. The night grew colder as we waited by the cars, shivering in our stupid costumes. Most of the trick or treaters were home, feasting on their spoils. Our mothers asked, "Where is his family? Where will he go on such a cold night?" Our fathers said, "It's not right to leave a boy all alone in an empty house." They were so upset they forgot to punish us.

We returned to school with our heads low, dwelling on the past few weeks. The previous night had left us in a dazed state. Around us, the other students congregated in their usual hierarchies. They were all preoccupied, aloof, talking amongst themselves in heavy overtones. They acted like they knew something we didn't. Gossip traveled fast in our town.

Over morning announcements, Principal Whately addressed us in her chalky smoker's voice. She explained a local boy had gone missing. Anyone with information was encouraged to come forward. Our classmates nodded to each other and continued to whisper. All day the chatter continued. No one knew the full story, but enough of the details. They knew about the house and the park. They knew that the builder's daughter was involved. In the end they seemed delighted that something had finally happened.

In Latin class, Margot's desk was empty. As we took our seats we realized how anxious we were to speak with her. Would her father change his mind and press charges? What had she told him about us, the games, about the boy we made up? She didn't return the next day or the next. Without her we lost our appetite for Latin altogether. Mrs. Burkett struggled to keep our attention and, much to her discomfort, only Benny Robertson raised his hand.

Jonathan Harper

"I know this is a rough time," she finally said. "It's horrible to lose a friend under these circumstances. So, let's take this week easy and just get through the lessons." We thought she meant Margot. Apparently she did not.

Later, we learned our parents had filed a missing-person report and were assured the police would take the matter seriously. Not that they mentioned this to us. We were still young, emotionally fragile and susceptible to danger. We read about it in *The Henderson Herald*. They ran a cover story about the craftsman house, the developers and the break-ins. That was the first of many times we saw Jonas's name in print. The newspaper published article after article and sold a lot of ads. In church, a plump woman in a canary-yellow pantsuit stood behind the pulpit. She commanded us to pray for his safe return. Even the local tavern held a fundraiser, though no one really knew what they did with all the money.

The following week the investigator arrived like an uninvited guest. His presence unnerved us. In an assembly, he addressed us in a dull monotone voice, detailing the sad plight of teenage runaways and abducted children. He wandered the halls in his gray trench coat, his righteousness steaming off him. We averted our eyes as he passed us by. He didn't seem to notice. Instead he interviewed the upcoming valedictorian, the football quarterback, the student-body president — only the kids who would have known Jonas. He didn't ask us any questions. In fact, no one did. We had been effectively stricken from the record. After a few days we didn't see him anymore. He might have figured it all out, that there was no point searching for a person who didn't exist. Maybe the town realized it, too, because people didn't quit talking about the disappearance — they forgot about it altogether.

*U*ntil December, when somebody found the body.

It happened over the winter break, after the ice storm knocked out power for two miserably cold days. We overheard the reports as our parents sat in front of the news. Some dog walker in Cavalier Park had stumbled upon him, laid out under the frost-coated branches of a pine tree: a young man about fifteen years of age, olive complexion and dark curly hair. Hypothermia, said the newscasters. They speculated he was homeless and had died during the storm. The newspaper ran a grainy picture for its front page story but as we reached for it our parents snatched it away. "Don't worry about that," they said, patting our hands. They underestimated us. We were observers,

sponges for information, and we knew how to use the internet. We knew instantly what name the reports were using: Jonas.

All of Henderson took the news like a punch in the gut. For a day or two the neighborhoods went silent through the slow thaw of the storm as people sullenly trashed their Christmas trees earlier than usual. The town hall assembly was the worst kept secret. Our parents disappeared for a few hours and returned home muttering to themselves. We were dragged by our wrists to the New Year's Eve festivities, held annually along the town square. Somehow, in the dwindling crowd, we found each other, huddled by the frozen water fountain while our parents drank mulled wine and discussed the tragedy. Children scattered about in their boisterous play, hurling ice pellets, blowing out breath clouds and playing with their sparklers. Little by little people left early, adults hunting down their young, and the town square was deserted before ten with no reason to set off the chimes at midnight.

New Year's Day, a town-wide curfew went into effect. All unaccompanied minors had to be indoors by sundown, much too hard to enforce at this stage of winter. Not that it mattered to us. There was no point in staying out. There was no place to go. We still eavesdropped on our parents. There was talk of another investigation and then a memorial service. Some morbid part of us actually wanted to see a funeral, to see Jonas's name carved in stone. We imagined Mrs. Burkett standing over an empty casket, mournfully reading a Greek poem.

At school we were greeted by Principal Whately's omnipresent voice from over the loudspeaker. "Be home by dark," she commanded. We wondered when the school would realize there had never been a Jonas registered.

We could barely hear her over the chorus of chatter. Everyone was talking about the dead boy as if it were the only thing that had ever happened. They discussed him with the enthusiasm of a delightful mystery. They talked about the house on the edge of Cavalier Park, a place no one had ever thought to go. When they mentioned the unnamed group of teenagers who met there, their voices filled with envy. We exchanged dark glances and smirks, but did not say anything.

We saw Amanda Sharpe, a horrid pretty girl, stomping down the halls with her entourage. In between sobs, she told her friends she had dated Jonas the previous summer and could not bear the idea of his loss. Together we swallowed the urge to laugh. In the locker room we overheard Craig Morey mention he and Jonas had been best friends when they were little and later

on Peter Coleman angrily claimed Jonas still owed him twenty dollars. Then Benny Robertson, picking off the dead flakes of skin from his lips, said it was all a mistake — that Jonas was alive and well and he had seen him just the other day. That was until Leisha Malone publically reprimanded him for having no respect for the dead. That, and Leisha knew Jonas was a fallen Catholic and we should all be concerned for his soul.

The stories grew. Soon the entire freshman class could recount where they were the moment Jonas had died, the various circumstances in which they had known him, loved him, remembered him. There were candlelit vigils, midnight excursions to the park, all sorts of events we were excluded from. Our teachers were obviously unnerved by the stories. They forgot their lesson plans and fell into stunned silence. In response, the school brought in a team of grief counselors who annexed part of the gymnasium, setting up makeshift cubicles, and encouraged all students to make an appointment. Hannah Burns was there every afternoon, wailing loud enough to ensure we could all hear her over the bell.

If the rest of the high school was caught up in the fever of Jonas, then our beloved Mrs. Burkett was miraculously immune. She seemed unaware of the growing hysteria outside her classroom door. Every day, she greeted us with near manic delight. Her movements were still ethereal, her black dresses swaying as she pranced around our classroom. Only Benny Robertson brought up the subject. He told her he couldn't understand how she could be so cheerful when a student was rotting in the morgue. Of course Mrs. Burkett had a way of brushing such things aside. She gave a haughty laugh and said, "My lovelies, there are five acknowledged stages of grief: denial, anger, bargaining, depression and finally acceptance. It appears your fellow students have invented a sixth. Self indulgence." And then she picked back up where she'd left off.

*O*f course the town grew impatient with the high school's grieving process. Urban legends about dead boys were bad publicity for developers. As far as the city council was concerned, the children were no longer in danger. They said we were now the problem. Overnight the grief counselors were banished and the gymnasium returned to its usual sadistic mechanisms. Teachers were ordered to continue with the curriculum. An ordinance was put in place: they weren't even allowed to mention his name.

Without us noticing, construction on the Jonas house resumed. Demolition teams tore down the old post office, sectioned it off with a chain-link fence. Even the vacant lots around Cavalier Park were bulldozed for more Craftsman houses. We heard rumors of the break-ins and the vandalism. The *Herald* ran a story about a group of teens caught inside, holding a séance. The "No Trespassing" sign disappeared and was replaced every other day. Our group rushed after school through the park, hoping to leave enough time before curfew. Spray painted along the side of the house were the words: "Jonas was here. And we will not be silenced."

We thought Jonas would be a shortlived phenomenon. Our peers were simple minded with short attention spans. But the stories kept growing and the high school was drunk on them. It was no longer enough for Jonas to be a simple runaway who died during the ice storm. With each retelling his death became more grandiose. They said he was impaled by a fallen icicle, bitten by a rabid dog, hit by a car and left for dead. Mike Daniels claimed it was a drug overdose and Clara Harberson said she had heard that he was on the run from the law. Murder became a favorite theme. His head was smashed in by a lead pipe. He was strangled by his abusive father. Shot twice in the head. They continued to speculate in the most grotesque ways, as if wishing him alive and well so they could kill him all over again.

The school brought in hall monitors, old ladies dressed in polka-dot muu-muus. Their task was to suppress the chatter. They lurked in pairs and eavesdropped. They stood sentinel by our lockers, waded in between cafeteria tables, armed with rulers to slap at those who mentioned the name. As soon as they passed, some brave troublemaker would hiss the word "Jonas" and the old crones spun around, flailing their arms, searching for the culprit.

Someone created a website detailing the many theories about the dead boy. They called it a conspiracy. We found Reggie Guntherson distributing tradable "Who Killed Jonas" cards that he had made on his computer. They were crudely printed with bad art and listed the suspects, locations and manners of his death. It didn't take the hall monitors long. All the cards were confiscated within a day. Then Reggie died a few weeks later over Spring Break. It was a car accident, one of those brutal wrecks that smashes a body beyond recognition. And that wasn't enough for a single lit candle.

Jonas became a ghost story used to frighten our young and gullible. How many times had we told the tale? Don't walk through Cavalier Park at night or else he will come for you. Entire sleepovers were dedicated to summoning

him through Ouija boards, all the players insisting they hadn't moved the pointer. Some claimed you could raise his ghost in the mirror by saying his name three times: Jonas, Jonas, Jonas. Our younger siblings went through a phase when they couldn't use the bathroom with the door closed. We'd walk by and see them squatting on the toilet, refusing to look towards the vanity. Disgusted, we'd slam the door shut and hold it tight while they screamed in terror, pulling against the knob, leaving soft trails of shit behind them.

Towards the end of freshman year, as the Memorial Day parade approached, the theater club announced the theme of their float: the Life and Death of Jonas. They did so early to prevent competition from the jazz ensemble, the student socialist party and the horticulturist club. But the city council put an end to that. They said they'd sure enough cancel the whole damn thing before they would let us go on promoting dead runaways. We didn't know what that meant or what was at stake. Many of us said we would boycott the parade altogether and yet, like every year, we all showed up along the main drag, stuck to our parents' sides.

We watched the long processional flow down Main Street: decorated cars and crappy floats, local business owners handing out coupons. The mayor and his wife rode in the back of a pickup truck, waving like royalty. As the high school band approached the center of town, we thought this was it: the grand finale and the end to another ridiculous parade. But suddenly the band stopped, halted in place, and left a startling quiet over the crowd. Our parents looked unnerved. Then one lone trumpet player started up with the military taps and from the crowds marched a group of black-garbed teens carrying a long black coffin. They were led by Mrs. Burkett herself, dressed up as a grieving mother. And from the stands and street corners came the council members and their crony police officers, ready to break up the trouble. The teenagers were prepared, calmly placed their fake coffin down, and braced themselves for combat. When the riot broke out, the police twirled old-fashioned batons and the marching band fought them off with clarinets and drumsticks. Even Mrs. Burkett was seen tackling Principal Whately as the crowds rallied and smashed windows and set the city hall on fire. And amidst the chaos the coffin's lid popped open and out jumped Benny Robertson, who ran screaming down the street.

Or maybe I dreamed up that last part and the parade finished without interruption. Maybe that's how I wanted it all to end. Maybe I had

overhead several kids at school talking about such a stunt but knew none of them had the guts. Maybe these were the same kids who whispered insults as I passed them by. Maybe some of them used to be my friends. Maybe we were once called wallflowers by our eccentric Latin teacher and for a while that meant we were connected. Maybe we never really liked each other. Or maybe we did until we became just as shortsighted as everyone else.

Here is what I know: Jonas made a good distraction, but he couldn't last forever. I don't know what happened with the police investigation or the memorial service, but apparently both things did occur before being erased from public knowledge. Eventually Eventually, Henderson simmered down to its usual tepid pace. The adults maintained their authority and teenagers stayed self-absorbed, only now there was an increased sense of distrust between them. The real tragedy, at least from my perspective, was after we were expelled from the house and the rumors began, my group never met up again. We created Jonas and in the end he was our destroyer. One by one my friends were absorbed into the Amanda Sharpes and Craig Moreys and Peter Colemans until they were all indistinguishable from them. They kept adding to the myths, adding so many lies that they probably couldn't remember the humble truths. It was enough to purge us of each other until suddenly I found myself standing alone, quietly judging as they pretended I wasn't even there.

In those last few weeks of freshman year, when students were burning out and cutting school, I maintained the same indifference I always had. I kept my head low, studied hard and when the bell rang I rushed straight home without a word to anyone. Except one afternoon, I lingered too long after Latin class and found myself alone with Mrs. Burkett. It was my first private conversation with this strange woman, who wore costume jewelry and loved dead languages. She lavished her affections on me, insisting I take her intermediate course next year. She said I was her favorite student. I thought, Why? She didn't know a thing about me. Like the fact that I loved astronomy and slasher flicks, that I suffered night terrors and still wet the bed, that when I got too big and my uncle quit our secret wrestling matches, I actually missed them. I don't know why any of this was important, but I wanted her to know something.

"There was never any Jonas," I said. "I should know. I was actually there. We made him up."

She didn't even flinch. "Of course he's real. He's real because people wanted to believe in him." I called her nuts, but still agreed to take her class next year and left the room feeling oddly at peace.

In the hall I stumbled upon the impervious Benny Robertson. He stood alone, leaning against his locker with his head bowed, as if he was patiently waiting for someone to come collect him. For the first time, I felt nothing but empathy for him and, against all rational thought, decided to make him my friend. As we walked home through uncertain territory, other students coldly remarked that of course the two of us had ended up together. And yet, when we reached my door, Benny was still beside me, smiling. We spent our weekends avoiding our families, watching anime films, crafting plotlines for comic books we would never draw. We confessed every embarrassing thought in our head. Together we quit the confirmation classes at church and, much to our parents' chagrin, announced that we were atheists. We found others like us, experimented with Dungeons and Dragons and circle jerks. Eventually Benny became my first lover. It was a doomed relationship from the start, but one that I would return to at various stages of my life. Even as grown men we joked that we were the perfect mates as long as we never saw each other.

I never told Benny or our new friends about my role in Jonas's creation. That was one secret, unlike all the rest, I actually kept. I wasn't ashamed; I had more fun playing along. Whenever that old topic surfaced, which it did, we would lay out the theories like a deck of cards. Jonas was killed with a pick axe, Benny said. I heard they buried him alive, I'd whisper back. Gutted with a hunting knife. Throat slashed with barbed wire. Murdered by Mayor Thompson. By his evil twin. He still haunts Cavalier Park. Jonas lives, we'd both say and burst out laughing. And then I'd think, if you find Jonas, you should kill him. That way he'll live forever.

Montgomery Boys

The boys at Montgomery's were neither the best dancers nor the best looking. But they were young and slender and all of them hand-picked for the virtue of wanting to be something else. Every dollar tipped was a dollar towards their future. There were standards here: a certain caliber of character was required. A Montgomery Boy did not steal or use drugs. There was no dark room in this establishment.

You could say Montgomery's was a different sort of gentleman's club than its predecessors around the waterfront. The stools were cushioned in real leather, the bathrooms were actually clean. If you took a seat at the bar and looked up, you'd find some buck-toothed boy swinging his dick around while the bartender passed out cocktails from between his legs. If you tipped the dancer, then he'd happily tell you he will be a senator one day. Too shy for the bar? Then you sat in the back and boys delivered your drinks right to your table. They were encouraged to mingle with the guests. You could give them a little extra for the conversation, a few dollars for the taxi home or a little more to help pay for their textbooks. To show a little extra appreciation you could buy them a drink, but only the approved spritzers kept behind the bar. Because Montgomery Boys drank sparingly and maintained composure — a duty to others, a duty to self — what good was an entertainer if he could not conduct himself properly?

Bruce went to Montgomery's every weekend with a near religious devotion. He knew most of the dancers by name and could recite their personal histories. He no longer fantasized about sleeping with them; he felt he was well past that stage of life. As he approached sixty, age had morphed him into a lumbering Santa Claus: red-faced, jolly, and a very patient listener. The boys always flocked to him as if they couldn't help it. To Bruce they were all delicate, elfin, awkwardly beautiful and yet full of shame and charmingly oblivious. It felt surreal to be surrounded by young men at this stage of life. He had read someplace that the Roman emperor Tiberius had kept a pool of boys to swim around him. The emperor's minnows, they were called. Bruce had a more innocent interpretation of this — an old man revitalized by a pool of eternal youth.

But it was the façade he enjoyed the most. He bought the boys their spritzers and they whimsically told him about their great plans for the future. The boys were also terrible liars. They did steal and use drugs. On more than one occasion the most principled dancer had confessed that he could be taken home for a little extra money.

The exception was Lenny. He was the worst dancer of them all, the quietest too, and was on the verge of aging out of the system. His most notable feature, his point of interest, was his claim to having been struck by lightning. Two days before his twentieth birthday, on a trip home to visit his parents, hours after he had made love to a woman for the first time. He was in the shower, still feeling romantic during the peak of a thunderstorm. The antenna was struck and the electricity traveled through the pipes. His evidence was the scars. They feathered down his back, thin white lines shaped like roots, only visible from the right angle in the right light.

Bruce liked the way Lenny slouched on his barstool, letting his resentment roll off his shoulders. He always guarded his crotch and gave a stand-back-or-I'll-bite-you look to the more touchy patrons. Lenny never asked for a spritzer. The more Bruce watched Lenny, the less appropriate it seemed the boy should work here. The young man was obviously desperate for money, but acted with such defensive arrogance that he didn't make much.

One night when the bar was slow, Bruce waved him over with a flick of his plump wrist. He approached Bruce's table with his arms crossed over his bare chest, like a scorned lover fresh from a messy bed and ready for an argument.

Bruce smiled. "Why the angry face? I only want to buy you a drink."

"I don't want that crap. There's no alcohol in it. It's like drinking piss water."

Bruce felt his chest rise slightly. He was delighted by the response. When he tried to speak, the boy put up a hand.

"I'm not for sale, so forget it."

"I wouldn't be interested if you were." Bruce smiled before turning to another young thing who came toddling over. The new boy was an acne-scarred mess who compulsively scratched his bum and was more than happy to let Bruce order him a spritzer.

Jonathan Harper

$\mathcal{B}$ruce started seeing Lenny around town as well: coming out of the Uptown Theater; riding up the escalator of a Metro station; waiting tables in a small deli off Connecticut Ave. They never spoke. Every time Bruce twiddled his fingers at him or gave a nod of recognition, the boy would obviously flinch before disappearing out of sight. It became a marvelous little game. As Bruce left his office, he would constantly scan the masses for him. Sometimes he thought he saw Lenny trying on shoes in a store or slumped over on a park bench. On the nights spent in Montgomery's, he would subtly point at Lenny with a wink. "I got my eye on you." He'd mouth the words before guzzling down his cocktail.

$\mathcal{B}$ruce worked as an analyst for a government agency that he didn't much care for. Its only saving graces were his pension and lunches out with his favorite coworker. Sally was a plump woman in her late forties who did investigations for security clearances. On the surface, they were an unassuming pair of middle-aged gossipers. No one could tell by looking at them that he frequented a strip club and she had been cheating on her husband for years with a series of younger men. Every Friday they'd drink lunch and talk about their various affairs before returning to work slightly buzzed.

After a suitable amount of time had passed, Bruce insisted they go to the deli, even if the only thing to drink was iced tea. He even asked for Lenny's section, twiddling his fingers as the young man deposited their menus. Otherwise he focused on Sally.

"You have to understand. I realize now that I'm not capable of actually loving someone else," she told him. "I like sharing a home and all the domestic bliss, but once I'm out and about, I feel like a different person. Completely untethered." She described an evening spent in a hotel bar when a tourist had bought her a drink with unmistakable overtones. "Sometimes I can only think about the moment and who I am in that moment. It's not always a wife."

"And you went back to his hotel room, didn't you?" Bruce grinned.

"Of course I did. When I was young I wouldn't have dared. I would have overthought it and given myself a panic attack. Now I'm not as finicky."

Sally often dipped into these pungent explanations of her affairs. A great deal of effort was put into rationalizing everything. Bruce liked that about her. "You're such a slut," he whispered.

Lenny brought them their plates, polite and distant as ever.

"You should talk." Sally nibbled her sandwich and traces of lipstick stained the bread. Her eyes followed Lenny's slow self-conscious movements to the counter. "So that's your latest obsession. I knew there was a reason you brought me here." They were quiet for several minutes, both batting their eyes coyly at each other. Finally, she asked, "Whatever happened to Eric?"

"Eric who?" Bruce fiddled with his pack of Virginia Slims. Goddamn the smoking bans. "I refuse to try and help someone who doesn't take life seriously," he said.

"And where did you find him again?"

"Where do you think?"

"Must be an interesting place. A lot of odd characters." Sally shrugged her shoulders and sipped her tea. "Will you take me sometime?"

Bruce let out a snide little laugh, as if he were twirling the end of a villainous mustache. "Maybe. If you promise to behave yourself."

When he turned, he found Lenny watching from the register.

"So what do you want to be when you grow up?" Bruce sat at his usual table, twirling his martini glass. Lenny stood next to him, wearing a pair of neon orange shorts that obviously embarrassed him. Around them, Montgomery's was unusually full, almost suffocating.

"Everyone always asks that."

"But that's part of the game! You're contractually obligated to answer." Bruce heaved out a smoker's laugh and sipped his martini. Ever since Lenny started coming by his table, he drank more. "Will you let me get you a drink at least?"

"After my shift, when I can have a real one." Lenny went quiet for several minutes, watching another dancer lean against the bar with his bare ass protruding out. "Today I want to be a secret agent." He gave Bruce a goofy look.

"You're not even taking this seriously!"

"Of course I'm not, but it's a fantasy." When the bartender wasn't looking, Lenny sipped from Bruce's glass and scrunched his nose at the taste. "I like the idea of being the most dangerous man in the room. I like to watch people."

"So do I," Bruce said.

Jonathan Harper

"No, seriously. When I watch movies and stuff, I always like the characters who seem to know everything. The mind-readers and the psychics or the espionage agents."

"Give me an example."

"I can't think of one right now." Lenny bit his lip and glanced over his shoulder. It was his turn to dance next. "Professor X, maybe. Or *Dangerous Liaisons*. Glenn Close's character. She said she had trained herself to watch people and discover their secrets. I liked that." The bartender waved and right there Lenny pulled off the shorts and placed them in Bruce's thick hand. "Hold onto these for me, will you?"

On Lenny's last night, most of the customers were preoccupied with the fluttering pixies around them. He struggled for every dollar, impatiently bouncing on his heels, his arms above as if pawing at an unseen dangling object. It went unnoticed at first — the sudden jerk of his neck followed by the disoriented look on his face. After a quick twirl, his body slowed. It looked like a brief, tepid seizure, a moment where he seemed completely unaware of his surroundings. His foot arched and the second missed its step. Then Lenny fell forward into the arms of startled clients. His weight crashed onto his left ankle with a sickening crack and he howled sharply as the rest of Montgomery's froze. The crowd parted and assembled, pulled him up, but his ankle would not support him and again he fell. The color had drained from his face. And when they propped him onto a barstool he was on the verge of hyperventilation. Someone suggested calling an ambulance while the other boys desperately clung to their customers, begging them not to go. The bartender leaned over, speaking in a low voice, and then Bruce saw the ferocity in Lenny's face. The boy yelled, "Shut up. I don't want to hear it. This is it. I'm finished with this place."

It took Bruce all evening to have the establishment surrender Lenny's clothes to him. He had helped the boy dress out in the open, had pushed the gawkers away and after much debate convinced Lenny to go to the hospital. Time took on a grainy texture as they sat quietly in the waiting room of Walter Reed. But the nurses were all very kind as they took his vitals and sent him off for X-rays. No broken bones, only a sprain. Thankfully, the boy had insurance.

"Can I take you home?" Bruce asked. It was nearly four in the morning.

"My roommates can get me," Lenny said without a hint of thanks.

"Will you be okay?"

"Besides not being able to walk without crutches? Don't bother coming in for lunch this week."

"What about some money?"

Lenny shot him an angry look but said nothing.

"I understand," Bruce said and wrote his number on the back of an old receipt. "But if you decide you need help, any sort of help, at least you now have the option of calling me." At first he thought Lenny would tear the paper up, but after several moments of contemplation he shoved it into his wallet.

The sun was rising as Bruce left the city and made his way out to the suburbs. Soon the neighborhood children would convene down the street for the bus. He liked his quiet neighborhood, his modest house and garden. It was ideally juxtaposed to the nightlife in the city, both separate but equal, each serving its own purpose. He was exhausted as he made his way inside, collapsed on the couch without calling the office.

When he awoke, it was deep into the afternoon. The light on his answering machine flashed and for a moment, he hoped it was Lenny. Instead it was Sally, whose voice sounded like it was kept in a locked cabinet. "Where are you? We're all worried," she said. He erased the message and sent in a quick email explaining he had been at the hospital all night. Being a man of a certain age and weight meant that he was already susceptible to accidents.

The stairs down to the basement creaked under his weight; his knees grinded and resisted. Light creaked out from the open door to the guestroom. It was a small dimly lit room with scuffed wood paneling and dirty carpet. An old mildewed couch, a television set and a tight washroom all crammed together to form the congealed mesh of playroom and prison cell. Eric lounged on the futon bed, completely naked and thumbing through a magazine.

Bruce frowned. "You're a little sunburned."

"Yup. I've been hanging out in the back yard lately," Eric replied. He played with himself in bored fashion, his hand gently stroking the semi-hard slab of meat that drearily lay between his legs. There was nothing sexual about it, simply an old habit. Back when Eric danced at Montgomery's he had a lanky swimmer's body with a delightful earthy smell of fennel, and claimed he was a follower of Foucault despite not knowing much about him. Back then he stripped for tuition and for life experience; he claimed he'd publish books

Jonathan Harper

one day and his philosophies would be his legacy. Now he was complacent to a fault. His body was doughy and pale. On his most productive days he straightened up the living room and sat out back on the three-seasons porch to smoke.

"The neighbors didn't see you like that, did they?" Bruce asked.

"Relax, I was wearing shorts. Nobody can see me anyway." He lazily scratched his belly. "I'm hungry, Bruce. My stomach hurts real bad and there aren't any eggs left or anything."

"Well, it's rush hour. Not a good time for grocery shopping, but there might be enough trimmings for salad."

"Pasta?" Eric asked.

Bruce laughed heartily. "That doesn't sound too healthy, does it? You should really go on a diet — what would people think if they saw you now?" He laughed again as the boy's face drooped into a pout.

"I want to go out someplace. Take me to the grocery store."

Eric sat up Indian-style and stared miserably. For a brief moment Bruce was overcome by the recollections of when he first saw him, recoiling one moment and begging to be touched the next. It was the same inertia that Lenny waded in neckdeep. Boys like these were the most charming and usually interchangeable.

"I am a little hungry. Perhaps we can go out," Bruce said. It amused him how easy it was to pacify his little stowaway. "You need to shower first and look presentable."

As he walked upstairs he could hear Eric already in the shower, singing a little melody he obviously made up as he went along.

There weren't many places they could go. Bruce had to choose wisely, someplace far enough to ensure no one would recognize them. A long drive was in order, perhaps to one of the all-night diners further down the highway. He'd buy Eric a few beers, liquor if they had it. And then he'd wait patiently for Eric to go to the bathroom and then drive off. It was the easiest solution. Far easier than what he'd gone through with Eric's predecessor. Then Bruce would come home and sleep soundly. Tomorrow he'd smoothe over everything with the office and he'd take Sally out for a proper lunch, someplace with a full bar. He'd wait for Lenny to call him — they always did. Then, after enough time of watching Lenny hop around on a sprained ankle, he'd make the offer and bring Lenny home. He would feed him generously until he

no longer struggled and then Bruce would fuck his mouth and offer all the guidance and protection a wayward young man could want.

The shower turned off. "Pasta for you, pasta for me," Eric sang out. "Add one more and then we'll be three," or whatever nonsense that came out of his head.

Tonight was the night. If Eric didn't go to the bathroom or pass out drunk at his table, Bruce would find another way. And then he'd have Lenny, his fourth. Eric skipped up the basement steps with such ferocity he might as well have tripped, fallen and broken his neck.

Bruce began to giggle.

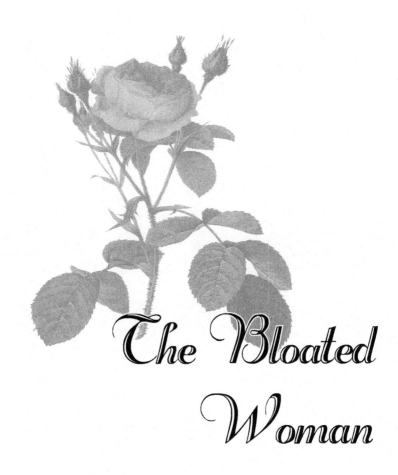

The Bloated
Woman

$\mathcal{I}$t is a strange story.

They discovered her washed up on the beach, her body naked and spongy, bloated with salt water. She was lying face up, the left leg delicately laid across the right, barely covering her pubis. The head bent at an impossible angle, suggesting a broken neck; her skin — the color of clay. If she had been beautiful, it was because of her plump breasts and stomach, and the luxurious black hair that was now tangled and seeded with dirt. Her body was meticulously posed, as if she had spent her last few moments deciding how she wanted to be found.

Every fishing town has a prescribed relationship with drowning: boating accidents, storms, suicides — Amos's father had worked on the trawlers for years and brought home the news of every one of them. At first sight, Amos discreetly pressed his middle finger against his thumb, a gesture used to ward away the devil. "Let's get out of here," he said, tugging at his younger friend's sleeve. "The tide will take care of this."

Jeremiah, however, was more naïve about these sorts of things. Earlier that morning he'd allowed Amos to lead him away from the boardwalk to where the beach bordered the overgrown nature preserve, where the sand hardened into coarse dark grains. Riptide posters warned against swimming; mosquitoes swarmed violently in little clouds. All Jeremiah wanted was a little blowjob or at least to see Amos naked. But instead they found the drowned body, and she was better than anything he could imagine.

He pulled away from Amos's grasp and leaned in closer for a better look. The drowned woman's eyes were cloudy pools of water. A scar was embedded into her chin. Sand fleas danced in the mass of her hair; she had not yet begun to smell. For a moment he was inclined to take a memento of the experience. Jeremiah told himself later that it was a clinical sort of fascination, that he was overwhelmed with his first sight of actual death. One is lucky if he stumbles upon a mystery in his lifetime. There was bruising on the base of her neck and wrists. A body doesn't wash ashore perfectly arranged face up. And then he poked her with a stick.

The police were summoned. They moved in quietly, as to not alert the locals, photographed her and covered her up with a gray tarp. A frumpy policewoman with her hair tied back in an ugly braid took their statements. Amos was short and curt and eager to leave. He had to be at work, he said. (He worked the night shift at the hotel.) Much later, when the beach season was over and Amos was finally arrested, Jeremiah would think of him in that moment: stubborn and angry and utterly useless.

But Jeremiah had no intention of leaving: he was twenty-five years old, still vulnerable to his own imagination and, having never seen death so close, was too fascinated to leave. Every detail burned into his mind as he watched them bag her, watched the body driven off in a dune buggy. Perhaps a little overeager, he recounted every detail (and added a few extra) even as the policewoman tiredly closed her notebook. "The bruises on her wrist," he said. "Did you notice the bruises?" She nodded.

"Where are you staying?" the policewoman asked. He told her the Lynch House. "Oh, the Witch House," she corrected, as if polishing off a dirty limerick. Then she was polite and insisted on driving him home.

*J*eremiah was a summer worker. He had met Walter Lynch several years ago, back when he was Professor Lynch, the flamboyant co-director of the college's philosophy department. As a student, Jeremiah idolized him. But now the title of professor had diminished and there was only Walter. Arthritis had warped his knees; dementia was warping his brain. That dazzling spark of brilliance had snuffed itself out and left behind the hollowed shell of a confused old man who constantly wandered off in thought and was unable to comprehend the simplest of instructions. Otherwise Walter was in decent health and only required a little supervision. When Jeremiah accepted the job as his day nurse he considered it a blessing: three months to repay his old mentor's kindness, with room and board included. It would also give him space to work on his novel and enough free time for a heavy-handed affair, the kind every twenty-five year old feels the world owes him.

As for the town, it was a fractured little community. Ever since the sea bass population decreased and the regulations went into place, the fishermen worked as if clotting a wound. The tourists kept the town's pulse steady. Boutiques and crab houses populated the old wharf, a new strip mall was erected by the highway and the only good beach, the one north of the board-

walk, was littered with white-trash couples and their over-indulged children. Every summer they bought and ate and watched the fishing trawlers from a safe distance.

$\mathcal{I}$t was early evening when Jeremiah arrived home. The police-woman drove without speaking, not even to ask for directions. The Lynch's cottage was a marvel of stonework and gardening with a large porch adorned with two Japanese lanterns. It was owned by Walter's sister, who managed a tea shop in town. The officer escorted him to the porch, where Nora met them with her usual pleasant smile. In the background Walter swayed in his seat at the harvest table.

"Where were you? I'm starving," Walter called out. His voice sounded like the coarse whimper of a mangled cat.

Nora patted the young man's shoulder. "Don't let him worry you. I fed him an hour ago."

Leftover pork chops sat in tin foil on the stove, a tub of apple sauce in the fridge. Jeremiah served up two plates and Walter greedily devoured his second dinner in a few bites. As the young man ate quietly, he watched the two women from the safety of the dining room. The officer spoke for what felt like an unnecessarily long time, careful to keep her voice low, while Nora's hand nervously covered her mouth. From the bureau Nora took out a small case of tea leaves and placed them in the officer's hand.

As Nora joined them, Walter stared at his empty plate. He had a look of bewilderment. "Something happened. Something went wrong," he said.

"Some poor girl drowned off shore. Jeremiah found her down by the preserve this morning."

Walter puckered his lips. Half-chewed bits of pork sputtered out of his mouth and dribbled down his shirt. Jeremiah, now by reflex, took his napkin and wiped Walter's chin clean. It saddened him to do so.

"What the hell were you doing down there anyway?" Walter asked.

"He was just taking a walk with Amos Moyer," Nora replied.

"Him? What were you doing with him?"

They all remained silent for several minutes before Jeremiah cleared the dishes and Nora put Walter to bed.

$\mathcal{J}$eremiah slept in the sunroom past the kitchen. It was a tight space with a daybed, given the illusion of expansiveness by large streaked windows overlooking the woods. There were many pretty things: lacy window dressings, shelves full of books and the half-moons of seashells, a painting of colonial ships hung on the side wall. He lay on the daybed, naked and sweating, watching the ceiling fan twirl hypnotically. He tried masturbating in slow steady jerks, imagining Amos undressing him on the beach. It didn't work. His dick remained limp in his hand. As hard as he tried he could not remember what had made Amos so attractive to him. Had it been his grizzled beard and shaggy hair or that fact that he was married and this was a gossipy town? It didn't matter. Jeremiah's thoughts were too staggered for him to sleep. He rummaged through the bookshelves and then spent an hour pacing back and forth along the white-washed floorboards.

Jeremiah's mind was laid out much like the sunroom, only a little narrower and over-stimulated with piles of junk. Walter and Nora were represented by the smallest fixtures. Amos was the daybed, awaiting later use. But the drowned woman existed throughout: in the cover art of the books, her body imprinted in the curtains and bedspread and every other fabric, other parts hidden in the overflow of papers and albums and little ornamental pieces; the amount of these only seemed to grow. She was the reflection in the windows, on the other side of the door, until he was certain that she was everywhere, holding up the walls to prevent the weight of her from crashing down through the roof. When he finally slept and bridged into dream, he was wandering the beach, looking for her in the waves. He awoke, hours before sunrise, morbidly alert and desperate to go into town and check out the aftermath.

*B*each towns are arrogant places. Unbeknownst to the tourists, each morning the wharf staged the disgruntled march of the fishermen, walking down its morose planks towards the marina. This occurred as the hotel graveyard shifts ended and the clerks stumbled out in their pristine uniforms. Both collectives never hid their disgust for each other. They were always on the edge of violence, muttering insults and empty threats. There would be no peace until the end of summer.

Jeremiah, however, had no interest in such rivalries. The march passed by without his notice. He chose a little café near the boardwalk where the barista nodded a sleepy greeting and poured him an espresso. She was an almond-eyed, mousy girl and smiled graciously as he dropped a dollar in the tip jar. The morning paper was deposited in a little tin display and he snatched one

Jonathan Harper

up. The front-page story talked about the possible demolition of a trawler marina to make way for the country club that promised to bring in more revenue. A poorly worded editorial by one of the dockworkers pleaded to lessen the fishing regulations — a small town must have its priorities. But the drowned woman was not mentioned anywhere. At first Jeremiah was disappointed. Then he was overwhelmed by the thrill of conspiracy.

Amos stood out on the street, wearing a pair of raggedy shorts and a tank top. "You look like a hobo," Jeremiah teased and the man shrugged.

"Not working today. I can look like a hobo if I want." Amos's eyes were a pair of murky puddles, dimwitted too. He subtly removed his wedding ring and deposited it in his pocket.

"The paper didn't mention anything about yesterday," Jeremiah said. He tapped a postcard stand with his fingers and watched it twirl. "Doesn't it seem odd they wouldn't put it in the crime report?"

"That doesn't surprise me," Amos replied.

"Well, it surprises me."

After circling the block twice, they entered a used bookstore. It was dimly lit, humid and cavernous, with large warped shelves overstuffed with books. The clerk, a plump sweating man with wire-rimmed glasses, tried handing them one of the various fliers that littered the counter. Apparently the bookstore was often overlooked and the man was hungry for customers and conversation. He was prattling on about some special deal and Amos slipped away into the recess of the store. Jeremiah lingered up front, browsing a display of dusty art books. He knew why Amos had disappeared, he was not naïve about these sorts of things — he was simply ambivalent. Then he realized the funny little clerk was still chatting away from behind the register.

"We got a great deal of those from an estate sale. Nice old lady, very sad. But if you're interested, I'll give you a price of them on wholesale."

"I just want to look around a bit," Jeremiah said and glanced behind him.

"Right." The clerk, too, was not that naïve.

The bookstore was deceptively deep; its shelves created a labyrinthine floor plan. Everything was covered in dust and smelled of old attics and cellars, the kind that had frightened him in childhood. Further back, some of the hanging lights were out. His footsteps creaked beneath him. From the shadows, he saw the flash of a mouse. And when he finally noticed the dark figure watching him, Jeremiah yelped.

Amos stood in an alcove, gave a wicked smile and squeezed his crotch.

THE BLOATED WOMAN

"Stop it. We'll get caught," Jeremiah said.

Amos observed him as if he were admiring a fancy trinket in a store window. When Amos reached for his zipper, Jeremiah nervously walked away.

The clerk watched as they surfaced from the stacks and Jeremiah plucked up a handful of books from the various piles. He settled on a paperback, a thriller about a serial killer, and placed it on the counter.

"If you like that, you should check out our local authors shelf," the clerk said. He placed another one of the fliers in the bag. "There's a good mystery series over there."

"I feel like I'm living a mystery. This place is like Twin Peaks."

The clerk stared blankly. "How do you mean?"

"Maybe not," Jeremiah said and turned to find Amos had left without saying a word.

*W*hen he arrived back at the cottage Nora had already left for work. His lunch had been left on the countertop but the sight of two dirtied plates said that Walter had eaten Jeremiah's share. Otherwise the cottage was disappointingly quiet and ordinary. The only signs of life came from the den's television and the coarse guttural noise of Walter clearing his throat.

However, one odd thing Jeremiah noticed: a small bowl of water sat by the front door. He hadn't seen it at first. It was a simple plastic mixing bowl right next to the umbrella stand — the water was lukewarm. Then he found another by the entranceway to the back porch and a third guarding the French doors of the sunroom. He picked up one of them and carried it to the den, where Walter rocked in his chair.

"Did you put this out?" Jeremiah asked. Walter shook his head, eyes focused on the television. "It's all right if you did, but be careful. I could have stepped in one of these."

Walter yawned in a mocking way. "She did it," and then turned up the volume.

Jeremiah collected the bowls and cleaned the kitchen. A few moments later Walter shuffled in. He was in a needy mood, every few minutes calling for Jeremiah's assistance. He couldn't find his reading glasses and then couldn't reach his favorite mug; he needed assistance rearranging the conch shells displayed in the foyer. Even when the doors to the sunroom were shut tight, Jeremiah felt a flush of aggravated energy when he heard the weak tapping against them.

Jonathan Harper

"Where did this come from?" Walter held up the serial killer book, his sour mouth frowning. "It's so morbid."

"This whole place is morbid," Jeremiah said to himself. He put Walter out on the front porch with the newspaper and a glass of iced tea while he mowed the lawn. He sat Walter back at the dining table while he cleaned the bathroom. The entire time his mind was on the beach.

$\mathcal{F}$or days Jeremiah wandered in and out of a state of half-sleep, that foggy space existing in midnight route between bed and toilet. He would jolt awake at four in the morning and before sunrise, having surrendered to insomnia, took sluggish walks in town. Nothing ever changed. The daily parade of dueling hotel workers and fishermen passed him by without taking notice. By mid-morning the wharf was animated with tourists. He considered venturing down the shore towards the nature preserve but never did. Occasionally he sat in the foyer of a hotel and helped himself to the continental breakfast. The staff regarded him with the same polite diffidence offered to a paying guest. Amos had vanished. Jeremiah looked everywhere and couldn't find him. Without anyone else to talk to, he was careful to return home before Nora left for work. There he fed Walter and kept the cottage in pristine condition. Still he would find the little bowls of water resting in a doorway. He resented them, eyed them suspiciously, cleaned out each one and replaced them in the cupboard. And yet they would reappear the next day. He avoided Walter as much as possible.

$\mathcal{S}$ometimes he wondered if this summer was all a mistake. He had always liked the idea of independence and seclusion but the actuality of it never matched what he envisioned. It was easy to forget that he had wanted to finish his novel, that he had come to this beach town for inspiration. Instead his work sat abandoned on the sunroom's desk, over two hundred loose sheets of handwritten scribble. He'd been writing it for years, in small uncontrolled bursts, adding one section at a time, even though he no longer remembered the plot. But he felt compelled to continue. When he did thumb through the pages, he could recall a specific afternoon, years ago, in Walter's office, surrounded by historic texts and abstract paintings. Both of them were slightly disheveled. Professor Lynch adjusted his tie before retrieving the handful of crumpled papers from the top desk drawer. "The question you need to ask yourself is am I writing about a life? Or telling the story of a life?" It was the last sensible thing Walter ever said to him.

Under the twirling fan of the sunroom Jeremiah glanced over his work and sighed. One thing he was certain of, it was based on his own life and that wasn't good enough. He stayed up all night rereading, rethinking, until he surrendered to the daybed and that tedious shallow sleep that never lasted long enough.

*O*nce, and only once, he went to the police station. It was a small compact brick building with tinted windows. Everyone inside was idling or eating. This added to his impression that the world was oblivious. The receptionist looked at him with a blank expression and pointed down the hall to a small office. The policewoman with the ugly hair bun sat behind a large metal desk eating a croissant. She didn't seem to recognize him. "Oh, yes, you're the Lynches' border," she finally said with disinterest.

"I was wondering if there was an update on the woman I found," Jeremiah said. "There's been nothing in the paper. Was she ever identified?"

The officer clasped her hands together like a bishop and shook her head. There were numerous files covered with crumbs under her elbows.

"You'll keep me posted, won't you?"

"Of course," she said in a flat voice. She thanked him for his concern and escorted him to the door. He left feeling pushed out.

*A*nother week of sleepless nights passed and his tendons hurt; dark rings encircled his eyes. It was past midnight when Nora came through the French doors of the sunroom, giving enough pause for Jeremiah to cover himself with a sheet. She held a large clay teacup, filled with tepid water and blossoms floating on the surface.

"I thought you might be up. Don't drink this too fast. It's potent." She sat on the edge of the mattress as he took a sip. It tasted bitter at first, but soothed with honey. Nora smiled as if wanting to stroke his hair. "I appreciate all the help, really I do. But it can't be good for a young man to spend so much time alone."

"I've had stuff on my mind," he said. Suddenly he felt drowsy.

"Yes, Amos Moyer, I presume." She glanced back to make sure the doors were shut. "He's a very nice man. But he's been taking young men like you down by the woods for years. Never keeps them long after." She took the

Jonathan Harper

mug and cocked her head. She had given him a secret. He drifted into sleep and did not remember her leaving the room.

That night, when he dreamed, it wasn't about the drowned woman but of looking for her. He walked the beach at dusk. He searched the woods, tripping over roots and pushing through thorn bushes. He finally dove out against the rough waves only to be shoved back ashore. And when he awoke, well after sunrise, light framed the daybed. It was the best sleep he'd had all summer and he felt anxious to walk into town.

The arch of the summer brought on a heatwave that made the fish market stink for three days straight. Nora made seared scallops with turnip greens and baked salmon casseroles. One morning Jeremiah caught her placing a bowl of water outside his door. She gave a little cackle and said, "Oh, just a little trick to catch wayward spirits. We all have our silly habits." On occasion she asked Jeremiah to take Walter on walks along the strip. They forced him to wear a neon-green jacket that embarrassed him. He only wandered off once but Jeremiah spotted him admiring two children running a kite, a giant glowing lime in a crowd of burnt skin. In his spare time Jeremiah stayed on the north beach to swim or in the café working on the novel. Some days he was productive, others he was not. A happy couple from Boston shared drinks with him at one of the bars. He visited the bookstore clerk and purchased the mystery novels he recommended.

When Amos finally reappeared, it unlocked a little door in the back of Jeremiah's mind. It was nearly dusk and Amos stood on the boardwalk waving a hand. It surprised Jeremiah enough to make him nearly trip over his own feet. There was no explanation for his absence, just his warm smile, greeting Jeremiah the way one does a beloved friend. Somewhere along the way Amos's smile turned venomous. Jeremiah saw him pull his wedding ring off and slip it into his pocket.

"Let's go for a walk on the beach," Amos said.

"No, thank you. I've already been there today."

"Let's go catch the sunset."

"Actually, I'm hungry. You can join me for dinner if you like." Jeremiah said this with trepidation, half-expecting Amos to give some fickle excuse and wander off into the crowd. Though Amos frowned, he agreed as if it were easier to do than not.

They chose a diner near the highway. Nautical props were strewn about in a vain attempt at ambiance: pieces of netting hung from the countertops, a replica of a ship anchor was positioned by the doorway. Tourists often ignored the diner but the locals loved it. Amos chose a booth up front and they sat quietly. Soon they realized they had little to say, the conversation limited to their mutual hatred of country music and unruly children. The waitress brought them platters of greasy fries and open-faced sandwiches, her eyebrow raised in a knowing manner.

"Did the police ever visit you?" Jeremiah asked in a weak voice. It had taken him some time to build up the courage.

Amos slurped his milkshake. An eyebrow cocked and his hands fidgeted over his cigarette case. Then Jeremiah regretted the question. "Yes. That lovely woman came by once during my shift and asked a few questions."

"What did she say?"

"She said you and I are the prime suspects and we'll be arrested for murder as soon as she gets enough evidence." Amos presented his hands for a pair of invisible handcuffs. Then he slumped further into the booth and sucked down the remainder of his milkshake.

"Seriously, did they ever find out who she was? I couldn't get any information anywhere," Jeremiah continued. He glanced around the diner. A trio of fishermen sat grumbling at the counter. Their hands were ugly and lacerated. Their musky odors carried all the way to the booth. "I had trouble sleeping at night for a while. It was a strange feeling."

"When are you gonna stop being a drag and start being fun again?" Amos grumbled. He returned a nod of recognition to one of the men at the counter. For a moment it seemed like their booth had been under observation for a long time.

"She could have been anybody. Somebody's wife. Your wife."

"That's not funny."

The room went silent as the jukebox switched records. In that moment Jeremiah knew that if he didn't say something, something witty or profound, the conversation would permanently end. A day ago he wouldn't have cared. Now it meant everything. His foot lifted under the table and grazed against the seams of Amos's thigh.

"Don't do that here," Amos said in a harsh whisper. He pushed out of the booth with his cigarette case and sauntered outside. At another table a man blew a wet sneeze into a napkin, but otherwise the diner went quiet with the

exception of the jukebox. Jeremiah counted the bills in his wallet, hoping he had enough to cover their tab.

*W*hat keeps a young man stagnant in a restaurant booth after he's been left behind? The rest of the summer could be measured in trips to the diner. Sometimes Amos was there, other times not. Their affair had been brief and unfulfilling. Jeremiah determined to rid himself of Amos for good, but never did. They met several times, none of them as thrilling as the first.

For Jeremiah, the diner became his only place of solace. He preferred it to the wharf because of its seclusion. He went there almost every day, bringing his books and papers. The waitresses greeted him by name; the locals minded their own business. Sitting in the same booth, he trashed the novel, that juvenile attempt at greatness. For days he pondered over empty pages of a spiral notebook and then began to write about a bloated body that washed up on shore. He named her, described her and detailed her entire history. He just didn't know what to do with her.

It seemed the drowned woman hovered everywhere in ghastly morning fogs and again in the evening tides. Somehow the insidious little town managed to cover her up and then refused to acknowledge her existence. The policewoman never returned Jeremiah's calls. Presumably the body remained unidentified and was turned over to the state. Then came the city council's decision to covert the trawler marina into the country club and that ensnared everyone's attention. Even Walter, sitting in his lounger, was inclined to long rants against the decision. Arguments were published weekly in the newspaper and protests from the fishermen offended the tourists. The tension continued to escalate until one night a collective of dockworkers disposed of the rotting scraps of the fish market in the public waste bins all over town. Everything stank and stores were closed for two days while the health inspector made his rounds. The point was made and the city recanted its decision. Beach season finally ended and with it went the hotels' summer staff. By mid-September the wharf was peaceful every morning.

Eventually Walter died from his second stroke. One night he simply drifted off into the fog of sleep and couldn't retrace his steps back. Nora mourned him quietly, sent notifications on little sheets of ivory stationary. The memorial service was held at the cottage and, for a few brief hours, it was wild with old professors and lovers and ex-students, before the cottage returned to its temporal quiet. Shortly after, Amos was arrested. He had lured a fifteen-year-

THE BLOATED WOMAN

old tourist boy down to the nature preserve one early morning. Though the details were vague, the whole town knew what had happened, despite Amos pleading the boy had lied about his age. He was handcuffed and marched up along the wharf, giving the newspaper its front-page story.

Jeremiah left before the beach season officially ended, returned to his old job and apartment. Everything remained the same, though feeling a tad more claustrophobic. The taint of the beach town quickly faded: his body turned pale again and slightly chubby. Soon he summarized the entire summer in a single sentence: "I spent three months in a little beach town and found a dead woman on the shore." He regarded Nora's letter with calm indifference, though his roommates, with their intuition for the dramatic, probed him for more details. He did not attend Professor Lynch's funeral (to his friends, Walter was still an exalted professor of philosophy and Jeremiah hated the idea of tarnishing that reputation). As for Amos, he claimed it was a brief forgettable affair, claimed they were only acquaintances and had no opinions on his crime. But if the accusations were true, then let Amos rot, Jeremiah said, and left it at that.

*I*t should be noted that Jeremiah met the wife. It was a brief encounter. She was tall and full figured with olive skin and long flowing black hair. What made her beautiful was her full mouth, her firm handshake, her intensity that gave all her mannerisms a sense of urgency. As Amos introduced them, he kissed her cheek as if to prove there was nothing to be suspicious of. She wasn't a fool. She knew her husband's habits of disappearing and the types of young men who kept him company. And when Jeremiah said goodbye, told her it was a pleasure meeting her, she was nothing but poised and restrained and shook his hand with a tight grip. He hoped to never see her again.

"*I* spent three months in a little beach town and found a dead woman on the shore," he wrote.

*W*henever Jeremiah thinks of this, he relives that night in the diner. Amos had stomped out because Jeremiah had mentioned his wife, his lovely wife, a plump Venus rising out of the sea foam. Jeremiah had assumed Amos would disappear again, perhaps for good. And if that had happened, the summer might have ended differently.

Jonathan Harper

As he prepared to settle the bill, Amos waltzed back in to their booth, the smell of smoke fresh on his clothes. He turned apologetic and cordial and even paid their check. When it was time to leave he squeezed the young man's arm in an affectionate way.

Jeremiah knew he should have returned to the cottage, but instead he followed Amos back down towards the wharf. They turned southward on the beach away from the strip as the sunlight receded over the crashing waves to their left. For the first time in weeks, Jeremiah's heart raced with anticipation.

When they reached the edge of the nature preserve, Amos undid his belt and removed his pants. His cock was short but thick and it burned as he pushed it against Jeremiah's backside. The young man was bent over, staring out into the white foam flooding and retracting over the dark gravel. Then the fucking abruptly stopped. It sounded like a ferocious little animal was burrowing behind him and a few seconds later Jeremiah felt a warm stickiness spray over him. All that anticipation for a lousy two minutes, and before he could even finish himself off Amos dressed himself and disappeared into the shadows.

When Jeremiah reached the wharf the evening sky was bruised with dark purple clouds and tiny blisters of stars. Tourists wandered everywhere. His shirt congealed into a cold sticky mass against his lower back and he wondered if the stain was visible. Up ahead, a haggard woman with leathery skin handed out small pamphlets with her retarded son. The boy was stocky and wore overalls and waved his hands excitedly as people passed. She managed to place one of the papers into Jeremiah's hand before the bookstore clerk shooed her off. "Repent," the pamphlet read in large bold letters. He considered tearing it up and tossing it behind him like confetti. Instead he bought a slice of pizza and folded the pamphlet underneath to catch the grease. Bar patios were crowded with drinkers and smokers; the boutiques changed their signs to "closed." A street performer winked when Jeremiah dropped a dollar into the opened guitar case.

It was late when he finally reached the cottage. The car was gone but the lights were on. Inside, a note sat on the bureau — Nora was out for the evening and had left chicken tenders in the fridge. The den's television cast an eerie glow and Jeremiah took the plate of cold meat with him.

"Walter? Are you still up?" he asked. Walter sat in his arm chair facing the TV screen and did not respond. "I'm sorry I'm so late. Are you hungry?"

Walter made shallow breaths, lips puckered like a dying fish. His eyes, glazed and foggy, stared back.

At first glance, Jeremiah thought he was pouting but quickly realized he was not. "Oh Jesus Christ," he said and the plate fell from his hands. He grabbed Walter's shoulders, gently rocking him, asking if he was all right, if he could hear his voice. Walter's neck bent over at an impossible angle and his eyes moved in rapid jerks.

Jeremiah called for an ambulance. The dispatcher's voice was pragmatic, his blunt questions almost insulting. "I don't know what's happening to him," Jeremiah said frantically. He pulled open the front door and turned on all the lights. "He's non-responsive. He can't even move his head." The wet sticky mass on his back seemed to burn like a guilty afterthought. And suddenly the words clogged in Jeremiah's throat. "He looks like he's drowning."

The ambulance siren wailed. It did not care whom it disturbed; its flashing lights made the neighborhood glow red. When the paramedics came through the open door they brought in their medical kits and a stretcher. They rushed into the den, where the television was still on. There they found them: Walter slumped in his chair with the young tenant cradling him to his chest.

Walter's body was heavy. Jeremiah wanted to speak to the medics but found his throat had knotted up. It felt like an albatross hung around his neck.

Jonathan Harper graduated with his MFA in Creative Writing from American University. His writing has appeared in numerous online and print venues. He lives in Northern Virginia with his husband, has a fondness for period pieces and really-really loves video games. This is his first book

Visit him online at www.jonathan-harper.com

CPSIA information can be obtained at www.ICGtesting.com
Printed in the USA
BVOW08s0207140715

408681BV00001B/25/P